JACKIE AND THE MISFIT PONY

J UDITH M. B ERRISFORD

Illustrated by Geoffrey Whittam

Armada

First published in the U.K. in 1975 by
Hodder & Stoughton Children's Books, Leicester.
First published in this edition in 1977 by
William Collins Sons & Co. Ltd., 14 St James's Place,
London SW1A 1PF

© Judith M. Berrisford 1975

© Illustrations Hodder & Stoughton Children's Books 1975

Printed in Great Britain by
Love & Malcomson Ltd.,
Brighton Road, Redhill, Surrey.

For Giles, Jessica, Katherine, Edmund, Huw,
Bridget, Oliver and Thomas

CONTENTS

CHAPTER ONE

WE MEET FRECKLES

"Here we are again!"

My cousin, Babs, spoke excitedly as we led our ponies out of the horse-box at the end of the lane that led to Pinewoods Pony Trekking Centre.

Below us the lake was sparkling in the sunshine. From across the valley came the bubbling cry of a curlew as the bird rose above the bracken-covered mountainside. Beyond the far shore of the lake was a pine-forest, dense and green, except where a stream tumbled and foamed in a silvery waterfall.

My grey pony, Misty, pricked her ears and sniffed the breeze as I saddled her. She snuffed the scents of heather, peat and pine and she jingled her bit as though she remembered the wonderful times that we'd had on our last visit to Pinewoods.

Babs' skewbald, Patch, was frisky too. He moved his feet restlessly, and the muscles rippled under his glossy brown-and-white hide as though he was glad to be released from the horse-box and to be in the fresh air again.

We said goodbye to the driver of the horse-box, strapped our bulging bags on to our saddles, struggled into our rucksacks, and, weighed down by gear, clambered on to our ponies' backs.

"What are you looking forward to most?" Babs asked as the rambling white-washed farm buildings came into view among the sheltering pines. "Seeing all the ponies again?"

"Yes, seeing the ponies, of course." I scanned the fields behind the farm for a glimpse of the trekking mounts, but there wasn't a pony in sight. The holiday season was in full-swing and I supposed they must all have been out on the job. "No, that's not quite true," I qualified. "I know I'm pony-mad but this time I'm looking forward to seeing Molly even more than the ponies."

I broke off, thinking of our auburn-haired pen-friend whose elder brother and sister ran the trekking centre.

"Me too," nodded Babs. "Last time we had to say 'goodbye' almost as soon as we'd said 'hello'."

"Yes." I straightened Misty's mane with my switch. "It was bad luck her getting chicken-pox and having to be in quarantine almost until the end of the holidays."

"Never mind," said Babs. "This time we'll have a chance to really get to know her."

I thought back over the exciting times that we'd had at Pinewoods on our previous visit, and which I'd written about in my story, *Jackie and the Pony Trekkers*.

I could hardly wait to get there again. Babs evidently shared my thoughts because she urged Patch to quicken his pace.

We trotted over the stony track and pulled our ponies on to the verge to avoid a muddy puddle. Then their hooves echoed on the plank bridge over the stream that ran down the hillside and crossed one of the grazing meadows belonging to Pinewoods.

Soon Babs leaned down to open the gate beside the cattle-grid, and we struggled to get through with our laden mounts. Misty's near-side saddlebag stuck for a moment against the gate-catch. Then we were through, and trotting into the yard to dismount.

9

We had arrived, but where was our pen-friend Molly, and the rest of the Collins family?

"Hullo," called Babs. "We're here!"

"Anybody at home?" I shouted.

Misty threw up her head and whinnied, as my voice echoed among the rocks beyond the farmhouse. There was no answer. We felt downcast. We knew the Collins family couldn't have put off the day's outing and disappointed the pony-trekkers on account of our arrival, but we did think *somebody* (perhaps Molly) would have stayed behind to welcome us.

We looked at each other. "What ought we to do?"

"We can unload the ponies and put them in the field," Babs decided. "Then we'll take our gear to the caravan. Molly's probably left a note for us there."

A few minutes later, we were humping our saddle-bags over the orchard grass.

We gazed ahead. There was the caravan, just as we'd remembered it, cream and green, with green and yellow striped curtains at the windows. We halted at the steps. The door was shut but, there, sure enough, pushed underneath was a letter— Molly's note, we thought.

Babs looked puzzled as she turned it over. It wasn't addressed to us. It had Molly's name on the envelope, and it was stamped and bore a London postmark. Miss Molly Collins, Pinewoods Pony Trekking Centre. Then followed the full address. It was written in purple ink in sprawly, untidy handwriting.

Babs happened to turn over the envelope, and before we could stop ourselves, we read something that was written on the flap—a last-minute message, apparently, put on after the envelope had been sealed:

Your new Dad's just come in. He sends his love, and says: "Cheer up!"

"Your new Dad," I read aloud, puzzled. "Goodness! I wonder if Molly's mother has married again."

"We'd have heard for sure if she had," said Babs. "Molly couldn't keep anything as important as that out of her letters. Anyway Molly's Mum lives in Birmingham, not London. It must be for some other Molly Collins."

"But it's not likely that there'd be two girls of the same name both at Pinewoods," I pointed out.

Just then Misty and Patch whinnied and we heard the clip-clop of pony hooves in the yard.

Babs and I spun round.

"Here's Molly now," I said, feeling somehow guilty at having the letter in my hand. "What shall I do with this?"

"Push it back under the caravan door," said Babs. "Then it will look as if we've never seen it.

We don't want Molly to think that we've been prying."

The sunlight was dancing on Molly's auburn curls as we ran to greet her.

"Molly, it's super to see you!" I called, dashing through the orchard.

"And it's wonderful to be back at Pinewoods again," Babs added, panting up beside me, "and, I say," she broke off to gaze at Molly's mount in admiration. "You've got another pony."

We eyed the strawberry roan with the white star who was nuzzling Molly's shoulder as she ran her stirrups up the leathers before unsaddling.

"Meet Freckles—a packet of trouble," said Molly, unsaddling while Babs and I talked to the pony.

"You don't *look* like trouble." I rubbed the mare between the eyes. "You seem a real fusspot."

"She's that, all right," Molly agreed. "And I love her for it, but she *can* be naughty too. She's unreliable. That's why she's such a problem."

"She must be, especially in a pony trekking centre," Babs agreed.

"That's just it," sighed Molly. "At first we thought it was because she was new and we hoped when she'd settled down she would behave better. We were beginning to think we were right because, for two whole weeks, she was so well behaved. In fact, we were all congratulating our-

12

selves, thinking she could be trusted after all. Then, this morning, it was back to square one again. She threw Susan and galloped off."

"Oh, dear."

I gazed thoughtfully at the strawberry roan who, at that moment, couldn't have looked more docile. For Pinewoods to have an unreliable pony on their hands meant that they would be losing money on her. She couldn't be trusted to carry any of the trekkers. Yet, at the same time, she'd be eating as much as any of the other mounts and would need to be groomed and looked after.

"It was because of Freckles throwing Susan that we weren't in time to meet you," explained Molly. "We were coming down to the crossroads with all the trekkers as a sort of welcome cavalcade. Then, with Freckles' playing up, it all went wrong."

"What exactly happened?" I asked.

"Something seemed to startle her. I think it was a yellow plastic bag stuck in a bush. Anyway she shied and wouldn't go past it. When Susan tried to make her pass the bush, Freckles started to buck. Susan went over her head. She had quite a nasty fall. While John and the others were fussing round to see if she was all right, Freckles bolted."

"Then what?" prompted Babs.

"Well, I seem to be more on Freckles' wavelength than any of the others," explained Molly, "so I guessed she wouldn't have gone far. I left my pony for Susan to ride and went on foot after Freckles."

"However did you catch her?" Babs asked.

"She didn't really need any catching," said Molly. "She'd gone exactly where I'd thought she would—down to the stream, and there she was, in the Fairy Glen, having a drink and waiting for me to collect her."

"It sounds as if, once she'd got over her fright, she quietened down and went to the stream for a drink," mused Babs. "I expect she was almost glad to be caught."

I nodded. "There must be some reason for her behaviour, though." I straightened the strawberry roan's mane. "I can't believe she's a vicious pony."

"Nor can I," agreed Molly. "I only hope John doesn't decide to sell her. I've grown really fond of her while she's been here and goodness only knows what would happen to her if she went somewhere else. Most other people wouldn't be bothered with her when they discovered she wasn't to be trusted."

Babs and I exchanged glances. We remembered Molly's big brother, John, from our previous visit to Pinewoods. He loved ponies just as much as we did, but he was the last person in the world to let pony-sentiment interfere with the efficiency and safety of the trekking centre.

Just then there was the blare of a motor horn. Freckles threw up her head as a red Post Office van came down the lane on its way back from delivering letters to the two farms farther up the mountainside.

"The postman!" Molly exclaimed, looking up eagerly. "I wonder if he's been here."

"Yes," said Babs. "He must have been. There's a letter under the caravan door."

"Just a minute."

Molly handed Freckles' reins to me, while she got the letter. She tore open the envelope, and took out a photograph and a letter.

She sat on the caravan steps, read the letter, gazed at the photograph and then, lost to the world, read the letter again. She seemed up in the clouds.

What finally brought her down to earth was Freckles dragging her reins through my hands and butting Molly's pocket, hoping for an apple.

"Oh, Freckles," Molly exclaimed. "I'd forgotten all about you."

Then, to our amazement, letter and photograph still in her hand, she threw her arms round the pony's neck, and we heard her say: "You don't fit in here any more than I do. We're both the odd ones out. We don't mean any harm but somehow we seem to manage to upset John . . . Never mind. What does it matter. We'll get by, somehow or other."

CHAPTER TWO

ON THE TREK

Babs and I looked at each other in surprise. Surely Molly couldn't really feel that she was the odd one out. We'd always thought of her as being perfectly happy, spending the summer holidays helping her older brother and sister, John and Susan, and their cousin Tessa, to run the Pinewoods Pony Trekking Centre.

That was how it had always seemed. Then, of course, I realised that, when we came to think of it, we hadn't really known Molly for very long. We'd written to her often, because she's been our pen-friend for a long time but we'd actually been with her for only two or three days at the end of our previous visit to Pinewoods because, before that, she had been in quarantine with chicken-pox.

"What did you mean, Molly?" I asked as she helped Babs and me to unpack and settle into the caravan. "About you and Freckles being the odd ones out? I could understand John getting upset about Freckles, but what are you supposed to have done? I always thought you got on well with him."

17

"I always did." Molly's blue eyes looked wistful. "Then something happened. I can't tell you what it is, because I promised John that I wouldn't talk about it . . . It's something rather exciting, really, if only John would see it that way —only of course, he doesn't. I suppose him being nineteen and me being only just fourteen, he feels extra responsible for me, especially when we're here at Pinewoods—him and Susan and me, with only Tessa to run things, and Mum back home in Birmingham a hundred miles away."

"Then, of course John's got all the responsibility of the trekkers and the ponies," I said. "I know Susan and you are good at helping him, but he's the one actually in charge. It's his venture and I suppose his future depends on it."

"Yes, he must have a lot on his mind," put in Babs. "That's why he probably seems stuffy to you sometimes. I expect most older brothers do."

"You've got us mystified, all the same, Molly," I said longing to hear more. "I can tell from how pleased you were when you got that letter that it must be something rather terrific, but if that's how you want it, all 'hush-hush', fair enough."

"It's not how I want it," Molly said quickly. "I'd love to be able to share it all with you two. There's nothing I'd like better because, in a way, it's really rather wonderful . . . only I can't make John see it like that."

"More and more mystifying," said Babs.

18

"For the time being anyway—" Molly broke off as we heard a clatter of hooves in the lane. "Here come the others. Remember. Not a word!"

When John rode into the farmyard with Susan and Tessa and the trekkers it was obvious that he was too preoccupied with pony affairs and the running of Pinewoods, to give a second thought to what Babs and Molly and I might have been discussing. As a matter of fact, he was a bit annoyed to find that we'd been, as he called it, "gossiping" with Molly instead of riding down to the crossroads to let them know that we had arrived.

They had all been waiting for us!

Then, when John found that Molly had put Freckles into the orchard with Misty and Patch, his impatience boiled over.

"That pony is a menace," he declared, exasperated. "I asked you, Molly, to shut her in a loose-box right away from the others where she can't do any damage."

Babs and I opened our mouths to protest. We felt Freckles might be an unreliable pony to ride, but we thought she wouldn't be likely to harm any of the other mounts. We must both have realised, however, that it wouldn't be wise to argue the point with John just then, so, after one look at his face, we exchanged glances and said nothing.

After all, John was in charge of the trekking

centre—running it was his career—and if he didn't make a success of it he'd probably have to work in an office in the town. Being an out-door type, he'd hate that. Besides, if we tried to stick up for Freckles just now—while John was so obviously only taking extra safety-precautions in everybody's best interests—well, he'd only think that we were a pair of irresponsible busybodies. Then he'd start wishing that he hadn't agreed to Molly's inviting us to Pinewoods.

As it was, he said firmly: "I could see you two were bursting to say something in Freckles' defence, but it seems you thought better of it . . . Well, there's no need for you to think I'm being hard on the pony. I really have got Freckles' interest at heart. If I let her carry on as a trekking pony, it'll only be a matter of time before she plays up again, and somebody gets hurt."

"Give a horse a bad name," sighed Molly. "That's all you've been doing ever since she came, John. Freckles has never had a chance."

"She had three chances," John pointed out, "and each time she let us down. If we let her carry on and some accident happens, we shan't even be able to sell her. And then she'll have to be shot. Don't you realise that, Molly? I'm trying to *save* Freckles from that."

"I wish I could believe it."

Molly turned and walked across the orchard towards the caravan.

John frowned as he watched her go, and then, to our surprise, gave a heavy sigh. He turned to Babs and me.

"Molly's having an unsettling time, just now, what with one thing and another. I hope you two will be able to take her mind off her troubles, and cheer her up."

"We'll do our best," said Babs.

"Good." John nodded. "Try to get her to join in the *spirit* of Pinewoods again. After all, we've got a super day planned for tomorrow. We're going to ride over to Llyn Mawr, cook a meal, have a sing-song by the lake, and then ride back along the old cattle-road to get home before dark. I've planned it because it's the kind of outing that Molly likes best."

Before starting out next morning, Babs, Molly and I joined the trekkers in the farmhouse kitchen while Susan and Tessa handed out the day's rations of bacon, sausage and tomato to be cooked in mess tins over the picnic fires that we planned to light along the shore of the lake, together with bread rolls, apples and oranges and a packet of nuts and raisins for every trekker.

John borrowed Misty who was standing with her head over the orchard gate, looking for me and inquisitive to see what was going on. He used her to demonstrate to the trekkers how to slip a rope halter over a pony's head before putting on

the bridle so that the halter lay snugly beneath.

He then showed them how to remove the bit, and to slip the rope of the halter under the nose-band so that the rope lay under the pony's jaw, before hitching it with a non-slip, quick release knot to a post-and-rails.

"Sometimes when on trek," John explained, "it may be necessary to tie up your ponies, so I'm showing you the right way to do it. Always fasten up your pony by the halter rope, and never by anything attached to the bit or bridle. Then, if the pony tries to pull away, the strain comes on the rope round its neck and not on its mouth where the bit might injure or frighten it."

He put a hand on Misty's bridle in order to demonstrate.

Misty jerked up her grey head and backed obligingly, and so the trekkers could see that John was right in what he had said.

"Make sure," he emphasised, "that any post or gate to which you may tether your pony is firm, because if the pony did try to get free and the wood happened to be rotten and broke, the pony might find himself with part of it loose and banging against him. Then he'd probably panic and injure himself."

He patted Misty who was enjoying being the centre of attention.

"Usually," he added, "trekking ponies are sensible, quiet animals because they are specially chosen for the job. You'll find that often we don't even have to tie them up when we stop to picnic at midday because we choose places well away from any traffic where there's plenty of space for them to graze.

"Our ponies have been trained so that we can remove their saddles, take the bits out of their mouths, and turn them loose to graze while we eat, without any fear of their straying, or being difficult to catch again."

He paused and looked round at the trekkers to make sure that they were all paying attention to what he had to say.

"Now listen carefully," he went on, pausing to

23

make his point. "This is important. I know that some of you have had experience with ponies, but you may not have had much to do with bridling or saddling ponies.

"Yesterday we caught and saddled the animals for you, but today I want you each to catch and saddle your own. Take a piece of bread from the bucket over there, and a halter from this table. Speak to your pony as you go up to it and slip on its halter. Then bring the pony back to the yard and Molly and Susan and Jackie and Babs and I will help you to put on its bridle and saddle."

It was fun to feel part of Pinewoods' pony-life again, and Babs and I were soon busy helping the trekkers. Babs was showing a shy boy called Robin how to adjust his stirrup leather while I went to the rescue of a zany, pretty-looking blonde girl of about seventeen who simply hadn't a clue.

At last everyone was mounted, and John inspected the ponies and riders to see that the halters were in position under the bridles. He checked that the saddle-bags of food hadn't been forgotten, and that everybody had their riding macs rolled up and firmly fastened to the D's at the back of their saddles before we trotted out into the lane.

Freckles, whinnying dolefully from her loose-box, disappointed at being left behind, struck the only sad note in the happy scene.

All the riders seemed light-hearted and happy. I noticed that Molly was smiling as, crash-cap half-hiding her auburn curls, she joined Babs and me in bringing up the rear of the cavalcade ready to help any stragglers who fell behind.

"It's going to be a lovely day," she said, patting the neck of the brown pony that she was riding. "I like it when we go to Llyn Mawr." She sounded eager and happy again. "We'll be going by the Miners' Bridge, and John's bound to call a halt at the Welsh Craft Shop, so that the trekkers can buy their souvenirs. He always does."

Across our ponies' necks, Babs and I smiled at each other. It was good to see Molly in such high spirits. Probably John was right, and having Babs and I for company would help her to settle down again to the Pinewoods routine, get over some of her excitement and accept John's decision on whatever he thought was the best for her.

Next moment our doubts were aroused again as Molly, her eyes shining with intrigue turned to us and said urgently: "Listen, in case we get split up during the ride, I'm going to need your help when we get to the Craft Shop. I want you to cover up for me. I'm going to slip off for a few minutes. There are two people I'm hoping to see, and I don't want John to know anything about it."

CHAPTER THREE

MOLLY'S SECRET

PONIES and trekkers were in high spirits as we jogged through the woods.

The sunlight slanted between the branches and dappled the carpet of pine needles on the forest floor. From above us came the cheeping notes of bluetits as they squabbled over nesting places or carried food to their young.

"Oh, look!" said Babs as we glimpsed a flash of russet. "A red squirrel!"

The bushy-tailed little animal sprang from branch to branch before disappearing into his dray at the top of a pine.

Yes, all the world seemed happy and bustling and I tried not to think of Freckles, left in her stable lonely and forlorn while we all set off to enjoy ourselves.

Meanwhile we were still mystified about Molly. What had she meant about Babs and me covering up for her at the gift shop?

Who was she planning to meet?

Why should she make such a mystery about it all?

Surely she would have to confide in us sooner or later.

What could it be?

My mind must have been wandering because, next minute, Misty stumbled, having caught her foot against one of the tree roots that grew across the path.

"Watch out, Jackie!" warned Babs, as I was almost pitched on to my pony's neck.

I regained my balance and shortened my reins to steady Misty. At the head of the cavalcade, I saw John bring his mount to a halt and hold up his hand to warn the trekkers to slow down as the path became steeper, zig-zagging towards the bottom of the gorge where the Miner's Bridge crossed the foaming river.

Above the roar of the water I heard one of the trekkers lift his voice in song: "There's a long, long trail a winding into the land of my dreams."

Everybody joined in, our voices mingling with the crash and rush of the river as it seethed through the rocks in the narrow gorge while our ponies picked their way cautiously in single file down through the pine wood to the Miners' Bridge.

John and Susan halted and told the trekkers to dismount and lead their ponies carefully across the swaying planks. As Babs and Molly and I went past, John called:

"Stand by, you three, to see that all the ponies

are properly tethered. We don't want any of them being startled by visitors or dogs and bolting on these slippery paths."

Babs and I were busy helping the trekkers to remove their ponies' bits and checking that the ropes of their halters were slipped under the nose-bands in the correct way before we demonstrated, as John had done earlier, how to tie them with a quick-release knot to the hitching-rail.

We were so absorbed in the job that we did not notice Molly had already slipped away.

It wasn't until John and Susan had inspected the ponies to make sure that they were safely tethered that we were able to clamber up the path to the car park and join the crowd of trekkers eagerly crowding into the souvenir shop in search of Welsh wool ties, pottery hens, spoons with the red dragon crest of Wales, postcards, films and homemade Welsh butter toffee.

At last Babs and I managed to get to the counter.

My cousin treated herself to a Welsh Lady charm for her bracelet while I bought a miniature silver barrel for Scamp's collar. My golden cocker spaniel was never far from my thoughts when I was away from him, and ever since I'd seen one of the barrels on the collar of a friend's cairn terrier, I'd wanted to get one for Scamp. The top of the barrel unscrewed and there was room inside for a fivepenny-piece and a slip of paper to carry his name with our address and telephone number.

I was just paying for the barrel when Babs touched my arm.

"Look, Jackie!" she said. "It's Father's Day on Sunday. Why don't we each send one of these?"

She pointed to a sign above a display of glossy cards bearing pictures of subjects calculated to appeal to men, like dogs, mountains, pine trees and heather, with messages "To The Best Daddy In The World" and other such glowing sentiments which we knew would make them laugh. Babs and I each chose a card for our respective fathers. Because Babs' father was a clergyman she picked one with a picture of a country church among the mountains, while I chose one for Daddy with a view of the Miners' Bridge and the rhyme: "Wish you here here, Daddy, dear!"

As I gazed at the wording my mind went back to the message written on the back of the envelope containing the letter that had been waiting for Molly on the caravan steps when we'd arrived at Pinewoods the previous day.

Your new Dad sends his love. Your new Dad, I mused. Yet it was almost certain that Mrs. Collins hadn't married again! Moreover the handwriting hadn't been anything like Mrs. Collins'.

When Mrs. Collins had written to Mummy to invite Babs and me to join Molly for the summer holidays at Pinewoods, her writing had been neat and round rather like a grown-up version of Susan's. The writing on the envelope yesterday had been untidy and sprawling.

As I puzzled an idea struck me and so I turned to Babs, and told her what I had just been thinking, and I added: "Somehow it seems that Molly's got *two* mothers."

Babs' eyes widened. "What are you trying to say, Jackie? How *could* she have two mothers?"

"I don't know," I said. "Unless perhaps she's not really John's and Susan's sister at all. Perhaps she was adopted by the Collinses years ago."

"I wonder." Babs' voice was thoughtful. "Yes, that could explain a lot. That's why Molly might have said that about being the odd one out."

"Suppose her real mother's married again," I speculated. "Then she'd have a stepfather. A new Dad!"

"That could be it," agreed Babs.

"Come on, you two gossips," John's voice cut into our thoughts. "Time to move off! The trekkers will need some help, and Molly seems to have wandered off. Be a couple of pals and see if you can find her."

We hurried off to look for Molly. The car park was crowded. Dogs were running about, children were playing ball and one or two middle-aged couples had set up folding chairs and were brewing a mid-morning cup of tea on picnic stoves.

Suddenly, a little way off, in a clearing I glimpsed two showy-looking horses in Western saddles and studded bridles.

One was a glossy black, about fifteen-two hands high. The other—a big, rangy chestnut—must have been over sixteen hands.

Standing beside them, their reins looped over their arms, were a boy and a girl who could have been sixteen or seventeen years old. Both were auburn-haired and both were dressed alike in black polo sweaters and jeans. With them, laughing and talking as if she hadn't a care in the world, was Molly!

As we watched, the girl was handing Molly a parcel.

"It's my surprise from all of us, Molly. Hope

31

you'll like it. My friend Gloria who works in a dress factory got it for me cheap."

"We had to guess the size," added the boy. "But I 'spect Gloria can change it if it doesn't fit."

"You're so kind to me," Molly was saying. "It makes me feel as though I really belong."

"That's just it," said the boy, as we listened in amazement. "You do. Blood's thicker than water. Stands to reason, Moll."

"And we've got to make it up to you for what you've missed," put in the girl. "Twelve lost years, eh, Molly?"

Just then the chestnut snorted and shifted his feet as if he was tired of waiting. Molly turned, caught sight of Babs and me and beckoned us excitedly towards her as if she wanted us to share her happiness.

"Prepare yourselves for a surprise, Babs and Jackie," she began. "Let me introduce my real brother and sister—Frankie and Debbie Rigby. You see, I was sort of adopfed by the Collinses when I was little."

So I'd guessed right! Babs and I exchanged glances.

We shook hands with Frankie and Debbie, and said how pleased we were to meet them.

"Thank heavens for a warm welcome from someone," said Frankie. "From the way her foster-brother, John, acted when he met us, you'd have thought we were poison."

"Moll was right," said Debbie. "She was sure you two would understand."

Suddenly the happiness of the scene was interrupted by a shout from John.

"Molly, Jackie, Babs! Where are you? We're all ready to start."

"Coming, John," I called quickly, hoping to prevent him looking for us and so stop him from bursting in on Molly's happiness. "We'll be right there."

"You'd better go, Moll," said Frankie. Then he turned to Babs and me with a friendly smile. "Take good care of her. She's the only kid sister we've got. Any pals of hers are pals of me and Debbie. So we'll be seeing you both. We're not far away. We're staying at the White Heather Dude Ranch."

"Keep that quiet for the moment though," Debbie warned us, and then gave Molly a quick hug.

Just then came the sound of hurried footsteps as John climbed the path towards us. He stopped in his tracks, amazed to see Frankie and Debbie with us.

"What's going on here?" he exclaimed. "A secret meeting?" He stared at Frankie and Debbie. "I thought you two were in London with your mother and stepfather."

"We decided we'd have a holiday near Moll," Frankie said. "Any objections?"

33

"Plenty," said John. "But I'm not going to list them in front of Jackie and Babs. They've only been here twenty-four hours and they seem to be in the thick of some intrigue. What have you been doing, Molly? Using them as go-between to give messages to this precious pair?"

"It wasn't like that, John," Babs protested.

"Of course it wasn't," said Molly. "Jackie and Babs have only just met Frankie and Debby. They didn't even know they were here."

"But *you* did," accused John. "And it's a bad show, Molly, going behind our backs. How do you think Susan and Tessa and I feel?"

"Susan and Tessa understand," said Molly, her eyes filling with tears. "They'd be willing to be friends with Frankie and Debbie if you'd give them the chance."

"Moll's right," Frankie said, stepping forward and glaring at John. "You're the only fly in the ointment, matey. Just because Molly's lived with you lot since she was two years old doesn't give you the right to boss her as though you own her body and soul." He raised a fist. "I've a good mind to teach you a lesson."

"Cool it, Frankie!" Debbie put a restraining hand on her brother's arm before the boys could come to blows. "We've got to see John's point of view as well as our own. I expect he can't understand why our family seemed to turn their backs on Molly in the first place." She moved to Babs

34

and me to explain. "Years ago, when Moll was a toddler, our Dad went to prison. Mum had a breakdown and had to go into hospital. Auntie Elsie gave Frankie a home, and I went to Gran. There was no one to take Molly so she was put in the care of the Children's Officer and he found her a foster home with John and Susan's mother. Mrs. Collins had always wanted a younger sister for Susan."

"Need we go into all that again?" groaned John. "For heaven's sake, stow it! I've got fifteen trekkers waiting down by the bridge, all ready to hit the trail for Llyn Mawr." He paused and looked directly at Molly. "Well, are you coming with us or aren't you? Make up your mind. I don't care what you decide."

Babs and I looked at John and then looked hopelessly at each other. We both knew that John really cared very much indeed. He was deeply hurt by Molly apparently turning her back on her adopted family.

"We'd like you to spend the rest of the day with us, Moll," Frankie said genuinely. "There's nothing we'd like better. We could all ride over to Celyn Coed and have lunch at the Bluebird Café, and of course Jackie and Babs would be welcome to come with us, too."

Molly didn't know what to do. She looked from Frankie to John, back to her real brother and then at John again.

35

"I'll go with John," she decided with an effort, moving to her foster-brother's side, half-turning to add to Frankie and Debbie, "I'll telephone you at the White Heather tomorrow. Perhaps we can have a real pony day with you then. And if John doesn't like it, he'll just have to lump it!"

CHAPTER FOUR

WHAT WENT WRONG?

THE sun was shining warmly, but for the rest of the trek Molly insisted on wearing the poncho that Frankie and Debbie had bought her.

"It's the nicest present I've ever had," she declared.

The misty blues and mauves of the Welsh wool poncho picked up the periwinkle of her eyes. She had a wistful look as she gazed at the path ahead. Was she wondering what the future might hold for her, and perhaps puzzling as to how she was going to share her love between her two families? It didn't make things any easier for her that there was such conflict between John and her real brother and sister.

My thoughts came back to trekking as, at the head of the cavalcade, John put his mount into a canter. Pony hooves thudded over the soft turf and I was fully occupied with trying to control Misty as Patch jostled past her in his determination to catch up with the others.

"Come back, Babs!" I shouted. "You know we're supposed to be bringing up the rear in case any of the trekkers need help."

Wayward Patch stuck out his nose and hardened his mouth against the pull of the bit. I could see that Babs was doing her best to hold in her pony but, in spite of her efforts, he was catching up with the trekkers whose ponies began to canter faster so as not to be overtaken.

Faster went Patch and faster went the trekkers!

The speeding up went right down the line. Soon the leading trekkers would be jostling John and Susan.

The middle of the ride was a bobbing, heaving, grunting mass of so-called "patent-safety" ponies whose long-forgotten coltish instincts had been awakened by Babs' headstrong pony.

Patch was showing his enjoyment at being back among the hills and heather of Pinewoods by indulging in one of his occasional bouts of unreliable behaviour. It was enough to make John ban him and Babs from the rides if he should happen to turn round and see the confusion they were causing.

I could feel Misty begin to dance under me. The excitement of the other ponies had spread to her. Firmly I held her back. Then I had another idea. Misty was a true Welsh pony. She had been born and bred in the hills. If I rode her up the bank above the path and cantered through the trees, I could overtake the other ponies without upsetting them. Then I could help Babs to get

Patch in hand and somehow halt the now rather wild progress of the trekkers before John realised that anything was wrong.

However, "the best-laid plans of girls and ponies go oft awry", as Daddy sometimes warns.

Misty scrambled up the bank and set off through the belt of trees at a gallop. Crouching over her neck to avoid being hit by the branches, I turned her to head off the over-excited ponies. Already one or two of the trekkers were looking alarmed. Sooner or later someone would call out in fright and then John would be bound to turn round and realise that something was wrong and that Babs and Patch had caused the upset.

"Come on, Misty."

I bent forward to whisper in my pony's ear, touching her with my heels to let her know that I wanted her to make an extra effort.

Misty responded willingly. We were ahead of the others now, and I turned her back towards the track. Next moment, the bank in front of us crumbled away in a mini-landslide. Misty pulled up with a snort and I flew over her head to land on the path, almost under the feet of the leading trekking ponies.

"Whoa!" shouted a boy-trekker to John and Susan. "Jackie's in trouble."

John and Susan pulled up, wheeling their mounts to see what was amiss just as the leading trekking pony—a stolid brown with one wall eye

39

—turned to block the path behind him and prevent the others from trampling me underfoot.

As I picked myself up and stumbled to where Misty was standing, looking woebegone beside the broken bank, the other ponies, with Patch amongst them, cannoned into the brown pony with the wall eye. A girl shrieked and Susan and John dismounted and came back down the path to sort things out. I quailed. John was looking very stern. He frowned towards Babs and me.

"You two can't even be trusted to bring up the rear. You'd better dismount and walk to the picnic site so that you can't cause any more havoc. As for you, Molly—" He turned to his foster-sister in annoyance. "You're not helping by wearing that poncho. It's far too hot to wear it today and if it flaps it may well startle the other ponies. Please take it off, in the interests of safety."

With a bad grace, Molly took off the poncho that Frankie and Debbie had given her, rolled it up and put it into her rucksack.

Crestfallen, Babs and I walked behind the trekkers to the lake. It seemed that our pony-trekking holiday, to which we'd looked forward so eagerly through so many endless weeks of school, was going to be blighted by John always being ready to blame us for anything that went wrong.

"Cheer up, Jackie and Babs!" Susan seemed

41

to know how we were feeling when we arrived at the picnic site while the trekking ponies were being unsaddled. "You'd better not turn Misty and Patch loose. They're not trained to trekking like the others and they might wander off. Slacken your girths. Run up your stirrup irons and knot your reins through the leathers. Then come and lend a hand with the camp-fire. We'll need lots of dry wood if we're to get the big billy can to boil for tea."

Babs and I found a super haul of pine cones for kindling and carried them back in our crash-caps. We were just about to roll some rocks into position to make a fire-place when Susan walked over to us.

"I've just been hearing how you met up with Molly's brother and sister—Frankie and Debbie Rigby," she said. "I've told John that I think it would have been better to have invited them to come on the trek with us. After all, they're Molly's family just as much as we are and it's best to accept the fact that they want to see something of her. It's understandable enough."

Even while Susan was talking, we could hear Molly apparently having a quarrel with John. Her voice was raised. She was speaking heatedly to him and gesticulating.

As we watched in dismay she ran to her pony, angrily dumped her saddle on its back, tightened her girths, mounted and cantered off.

"Oh dear!" sighed Susan. "More hasty words about something or other. Now I suppose Molly's heading straight for the White Heather."

"Or the Bluebird café," I said. "Frankie and Debbie were riding there for lunch."

We gazed at the blue waters of the lake with its white cloud reflections; at the black-headed gulls swooping in search of fish; and the tall pines fringing the farther shore.

"Wouldn't life be super if people could only agree not to upset each other?" said Babs.

However, even Molly's and John's bickering could not completely dampen our enjoyment of the day. Susan quickly had the fire blazing and we joined the trekkers in sizzling sausages, drinking mugs of hot tea and swopping camp fire yarns.

"They say Llyn Mawr is haunted by the ghost of a white stallion," Susan told the enthralled trekkers. "He belonged to a Welsh prince who was slain by his enemies while out hunting. The faithful stallion stayed out in the hills to look for him. Nobody could persuade him to go home. He lived, lonely and pining for a while and then, when he died, his ghost returned to haunt the valley. He's said to be still searching for his beloved master."

"It's even better than the story of the dog Gelert," said a sun-tanned, fair-haired boy called Peter. "You know, the one about Prince

Llewellyn who left his faithful hound to guard his infant son while he went hunting—"

"And when he came back the baby was missing," added Babs. "Gelert was spattered in blood and the cradle lay overturned on the floor of the cottage."

Peter nodded. "So Prince Llewellyn drew his sword and slew Gelert." He paused for effect and looked round at the other trekkers. "Then the Prince heard a faint cry from beneath the overturned cradle. He lifted it and there was the baby unharmed."

"But poor Gelert was dead," added Susan. "As a matter of fact," she told the trekkers, "his grave's not many miles from here at a village called Beddgelert, which means Gelert's grave. We'll ride over to see it one day and you can all read the inscription."

Yes, it was super, yarning round the camp fire but all the time, Babs and I were aware that something was lacking. Our friend Molly wasn't there with us to share it all.

"Perhaps she'll be at Pinewoods, waiting for us," I said, as we helped to damp the camp fires, scattering the ashes, replacing the turf and rolling away the stones before the ride back. "She could have gone home to keep Freckles company. I bet that pony's miserable all by herself."

Sure enough, when we got back, Freckles was waiting, her head over the loose-box door, gazing across the stable-yard to the lane. There was no Molly to comfort her. The strawberry-roan whinnied a greeting when she heard the clatter of the returning trekking ponies.

"Poor Freckles!" I said to Babs as we unsaddled Misty and Patch. "She just can't understand why she had to be left behind. It must have seemed a lonely day for her."

We turned our ponies into the orchard. We watched Misty and Patch roll and then start to cro, ⸻ atentedly. I picked an early wi⸻ ook it to Freckles.

"⸻' I sympathised, feeling the bru⸻ muzzle as she took the apple fron⸻ You hated being left behind, did⸻

⸻ in a way," Babs sighed, pat-⸻ ky-roan neck. "I suppose they are⸻ ut. I bet Freckles could make go⸻ tting, but it's true she's a dead los⸻ ing establishment."

⸻ led on the cobbles and next mo⸻ shadow fell across us.

"⸻," he groaned. "I might have kn⸻

"⸻ John?" I turned. "We're not de⸻

"Oh, no!" Molly's foster brother echoed. "Only breaking one of the basic rules of Pinewoods. Can't you read?"

45

He pointed to a notice tacked on to the open half of the loose-box door.

"DO NOT FEED TIT-BITS TO THE PONIES," Babs read aloud. "THIS MEANS YOU."

"Exactly," said John. "That notice is on the door of every loose-box at Pinewoods. You should know it by heart by this time."

"Oh, John," I sighed. "We'd forgotten. We didn't mean any harm. We're so used to giving rewards to Misty and Patch when we're at home that we just didn't think."

"You hardly ever do," said John. "But please try to remember that in any pony establishment, the feeding of tit-bits has to be banned. If the trekkers see you two feeding the ponies at any odd time, they'll start to do the same thing. Too many tit-bits means fat, lazy ponies." He broke off and looked at us earnestly and I knew that he was being strict with us for our own good and that he really did care that we should learn more pony-sense. "Tit-bits can lead to ponies becoming bad-tempered and snappy, too. They get to expect treats all the time and then, when they don't get them, they may start to bite and become unsuitable for trekkers to handle."

I nodded. Of course, John was right.

"Now, I don't know exactly what happened in Freckles' past," he went on, "but something must have gone wrong with her—something that made such a big impression on her mind that it turned her from the really first-rate pony she might have been into the temperamental unreliable animal that she sometimes is now."

"If only we knew what it was that went wrong in Freckles' life," I spoke my thoughts aloud to Babs when John had gone. "Then we might be able to help. Oh, if only we could."

"I wish we could help Molly, too," Babs sighed. She looked towards the west where the sun was dipping behind the hills that lay between Pinewoods and the sea. "It's almost supper time and she's not back yet. I wonder where she can have got to? Fancy her riding off like that without a word to us or anybody."

"I don't think she really enjoys being the centre of attention," said Babs. "Of course, it's most unsettling for her to have her real family come back into her life out of the blue."

I nodded. "Particularly as they seem to have so much money to spend. I mean, Frankie and Debbie are so carefree and unfettered. Their way of life must seem quite a contrast to Pinewoods where John has to watch every penny and where he and Susan have to give most of their thought to the running of the pony trekking centre."

"Not nearly so attractive," sighed Babs. "Or that's how it probably seems to Molly at the moment. I must say, though, that I wish she'd come back. She's not making things any easier for John by behaving like this."

CHAPTER FIVE

NOT ENOUGH PONIES

Dear Mummy and Daddy

I was sitting up in my bunk in the caravan and writing by the light of my torch.

When Molly turned up at last, she was covered in mud and leading Brownie. Brownie was lame and his fetlock was swollen and puffy. Apparently, after the row with John, Molly had ridden along one of the forestry roads, taking a short cut to catch up with Frankie and Debbie, intending to have lunch with them at the Bluebird Café. But a forestry lorry had come rattling down one of the steep side-roads and driven so close to them that Brownie had taken fright.

He'd shied and slipped into a ditch, tipping Molly off into the mud and then strained his fetlock trying to get out. So, not only had Molly lost the chance of catching up with Frankie and Debbie, but she'd had to walk, leading Brownie every step of the way back to Pinewoods. It must have been twelve miles. No wonder she was so late.

No wonder, too, that John was angry because, with Freckles condemned as untrustworthy and Brownie now out of action, Pinewoods is short of trekking ponies.

Of course, Babs and I at once offered to lend Misty and Patch.

As you know, we don't really like lending our ponies to be ridden by beginners but in this case there seemed to be no other course. Even so, John did not accept our offer at once. He said he'd think about it. I suppose he felt Misty and Patch weren't guaranteed patent-safeties like the rest of the trekking ponies and he didn't want to risk any mishaps.

I broke off and yawned. Babs and Molly were already asleep, so I decided to finish the letter to Mummy and Daddy the next night.

The following morning John came up to Babs and me while we were helping Tessa and Susan to prepare the breakfast.

I was slicing bread with the machine as Babs was pouring cornflakes from a giant packet into the rows of plates waiting on the long trestle table.

"I've been 'phoning round to see if I could get hold of a couple of spare trekking ponies," he told us. "Unfortunately there are none to be had. This is the height of the trekking season and everyone seems to need all the mounts they can get."

Our hearts sank. It seemed that we would have to lend Misty and Patch after all.

"Mind you," John said. "I'll make sure that they're ridden only by two experienced riders. I can see that you wouldn't want any ham-fisted beginners jarring their mouths."

"Fair enough," I said and Babs nodded her agreement.

"Oh, by the way," John went on. "I've invited Frankie and Debbie to ride over from the White Heather to spend a couple of days with us here. Susan and Tessa have talked me into it. I suppose it is a pity for Molly to have to keep going over there to see them when they could all three be having a good time here."

"I'm so glad, John," Babs said, her eyes shining with pleasure. "You're doing the right thing. I know it's going to be hard for you to share Molly with Frankie and Debbie, but—"

"Share!" John's echo cut her short. "You must be out of your mind, Babs, if you think my not wanting to *share* Molly is the reason for my not being keen on having her family round our necks."

"Then what is the reason?" I asked quietly. "Why can't you tell us?"

"Because I'm not given to confiding in little girls." John turned to the door. "But, since you want to know, O.K. I'll tell you this. There are a lot of skeletons rattling in the cupboard of the

Rigby family so, when you start getting chummy with Frankie and Debbie, just remember, it might be more tactful of you not to ask *them* too many questions."

"Skeletons!" echoed Babs. "I suppose you're trying to say that Molly's real family aren't very nice people."

"That about sums it up," said John not able to contain himself. "Dishonest, scroungers and in trouble with the police. They left Molly in the lurch when she was little. You name it, they've done it."

* * * * *

Were we supposed to dislike Frankie and Debbie, too, we wondered? If we did, wouldn't that make things even more difficult for Molly?

Besides, Susan and Tessa weren't unfriendly to them. They treated them just as they would have treated anyone else who'd become involved with the Collins family. Did John know something that he hadn't told to Susan and Tessa; or did they look at things in a different light from John, perhaps feeling that here was a situation which, for Molly's sake, had to be accepted, no matter how they personally might feel about the matter. Babs and I felt defeated. We just did not know what to do for the best.

"I suppose all we can do," said Babs, "is to

carry on as though we don't know anything about any skeletons in any cupboards."

Certainly we didn't want to do anything to lessen Molly's pleasure in having Frankie and Debbie to stay. Neither she nor Babs nor I could go trekking that day because there weren't any ponies for us to ride. So we spent the time together talking to Freckles and helping Tessa to make up beds for the visitors. Then, in the afternoon, we picked raspberries from the garden, peeled potatoes and sliced beans, carrots and onions to go into the mammoth stew Tessa was preparing for the evening meal.

Towards tea-time Frankie and Debbie arrived. They were still using their showy Western saddles and bridles and were astride the big, rakish chestnut and the well-bred black on which we had previously seen them. Behind them came the White Heather Land Rover bringing their cases and extra gear.

"Here we are, Moll." Frankie swung himself down from the chestnut and gave his young sister a hug. "We'll all have a grand time tomorrow," he promised. "And it doesn't matter about your being two ponies short. The White Heather can lend us a couple. I'll fix it."

By the time that John and Susan and the trekkers got back, Frankie and Debbie had settled in. They'd bedded their mounts down in the loose-boxes on either side of Freckles. They had

unpacked their suitcases and were in the kitchen,
Frankie in the rocking chair softly twanging his
guitar while Debbie helped Molly and Babs and
me to set the table for supper.

Everyone was in high spirits because the day's
trek had been a success. Tessa's stew was voted
excellent, and we all enjoyed the raspberries we'd
picked, helped down by dollops of fresh cream
and spoonfuls of sugar.

After the dishes had been washed we went into
the sitting-room and Frankie played folk tunes
and pop on his guitar while we all sang to his
accompaniment.

The trekkers seemed to be enjoying Frankie's and Debbie's lively company. It was as though their arrival had given Pinewoods a party spirit.

It was not until the following morning that a smoulder of disagreement arose to mar the general jollity.

I suppose it was the arrival of Firefly and Melody, the two ponies which Frankie had borrowed from the White Heather, that brought out John's half-hidden dislike of the Rigbys.

Like the chestnut and the black, the two new ponies—Firefly and Melody—were wearing Western gear, true to the White Heather's new image of "The Dude Ranch in the Hills".

"Don't think for one moment that those phoney Wild West broncos are coming out with the trekking party," John said as he watched Firefly and Melody being unloaded. "Pinewood ponies aren't used to strangers let alone hot-blooded, part-bred animals like those. We can't risk four newcomers. They might upset the others and so endanger the trekkers."

"In that case," declared Molly, "we'll have our own trek. Frankie and Debbie and Jackie and Babs and I." Her blue eyes flashed rebelliously as she faced her foster-brother. "I'll be glad of a pony with a bit of spirit, and some friendly company."

So the Pinewoods party rode off, with Misty and Patch among them, and Babs, Molly,

Frankie, Debbie and I were left with the four showy newcomers.

"Four mounts for five people," said Babs. "What are we going to do?"

"I'll ride Freckles," I offered. "After all, she's not going to become more reliable by being left in the stable, getting fresh, while all the other ponies go out."

Molly looked conscience-stricken. "Poor Freckles! Perhaps I ought to ride her because I seem to understand her best. But I was looking forward to a really good gallop."

"Which pony do you want then, Moll?" asked Frankie.

"Oh, Melody for me," said Molly, gazing at the beautiful palomino that had arrived on loan from the White Heather.

"And I'll have Firefly." Babs moved to take the reins of the bay.

"That's the ticket." Frankie put his foot into a leather stirrup and swung himself into the Western saddle of the chestnut he had been riding the previous day. He looked round at us all. "Now which way, pards?"

"Let's ride over the mountains," suggested Babs. "We can follow the old droving track to the Devil's Kitchen. I know the way."

"Not for me." Debbie looked up at the high mountains and shivered. "I don't fancy riding over those narrow tracks. I'm getting used to the mounted life but I'd rather trust my own two feet than four pony hooves when it comes to mountaineering. Why don't we go to Beddgelert? Then we can have a look at that dog's grave Babs was telling us about."

"Let's vote on it," said Frankie.

"I vote for the mountains," said Molly. "What about you, Frankie?"

"I'm with you," said her brother. "I'm all for hitting the old sheep rustlers' trail."

"Me, too," said Babs.

I could see Debbie's fingers tighten nervously on her reins. The idea of the mountain track really did seem to scare her more than the others realised.

"Why don't you three ride to the Devil's Kitchen, then?" I suggested. "I'll go with Debbie to Beddgelert. I want to get a postcard of Gelert's grave for my holiday scrapbook."

CHAPTER SIX

DISASTER FOR FRECKLES

As Freckles and I jogged beside Debbie and Jet, the black pony she had brought from the White Heather, my mind kept harking back to John's refusal to let any of the White Heather ponies accompany the others on the trek.

Was there really any good reason for it? Although the White Heather mounts looked showy and were saddled and bridled Western style, I thought they seemed really to be just as quiet and well-trained as any other trekking ponies. I wondered whether John's decision didn't stem from his dislike of Frankie and Debbie?

What had he really got against them?

Frankie and Debbie were both so thoroughly likeable, and they were genuinely fond of Molly.

Could there be any real harm in them, and were they truly bad examples to Molly, as John had claimed?

In what way could they have been dishonest? Had they followed in their father's footsteps?

Certainly, Molly's real father had gone to

prison and that was why Molly had been fostered in the first place. Molly's mother had long ago divorced her gaol-bird husband. Now she was happily married to a respectable turf accountant, or bookmaker, called Maxie Walker.

So what was John's objection to Molly's family now that their fortunes had changed and they were in a position to welcome her back to the fold? It wasn't as though they were trying to take her away from the Collinses. They just wanted to share her, which to Babs and me seemed quite reasonable.

I glanced sideways at Debbie. In her royal-blue corduroy slacks and pale blue sweater, with her fawn leather stetson tilted on the back of her auburn head, she looked without a care in the world. She was riding easily to Jet's trot and Freckles had to extend her stride to keep up with the black.

Debbie smiled across at me.

"Freckles doesn't seem to be giving you any trouble," she said. "I think it's a shame that John's got such a down on that pony, same as he has on me and Frankie."

"I suppose he has to be extra careful about any ponies the trekkers might ride," I said, not wanting to disagree with her, but, at the same time, partly understanding John's point of view —at least in regard to Freckles.

"Of course John's a bit up-tight about a lot of

things," sighed Debbie. "It's silly to make the kind of snap judgements he does in this permissive age. Just because Frankie and I've had trouble with the fuzz a couple of times, you'd think the world had come to an end."

"Fuzz?" I echoed. "What's that?"

"The law. You know, the police," Debbie said, shortening Firefly's strides to match Freckles' so that she could tell me more. "Why on earth anyone should make a big production about it—now that things are going right for Frankie and me, for the first time in our lives—I'll never understand. Anyway I'm certainly not going to be so hush-hush as to be ashamed and make a big secret of it all just when our family fortunes have turned the corner."

I listened in surprise. It seemed there might be something in what John had said about their being skeletons in the Rigby family cupboard.

"Our Dad—Mum's first husband, Syd— has never done an honest day's work in his life," Debbie was saying now. "Our Mum had a terrible time with him. He was always in and out of gaol. For years she kept taking him back because each time he'd promise to go straight.

"When Molly was two he got seven years preventive detention for house-breaking. That's burglary," she explained. "Then, a month later, Mum got busted for shop-lifting, taking food from the market for us kids. She was so hard up. She was fined five pounds but that wasn't the end of it. We had welfare officers in and out of the house every other day. That's when Mum had her breakdown and was put in hospital. The children's officer took over then. Frankie was sent to Aunt Elsie, I went to Gran, and the Children's Department advertised for a foster home for Moll."

"I suppose Mrs. Collins saw the advertisement," I said. "So Molly became one of the Collins family—unofficially adopted, I suppose."

Debbie nodded. "Yes, unofficial," she confirmed. "And it was Molly's big chance, so we'll always be grateful to the Collinses for that. If it wasn't for them I suppose Moll might have ended up like Frankie and me—on probation."

"Are you both on probation, Debbie?" I gasped, shocked. "Whatever for?"

"Well, Frankie got into trouble for 'borrowing' other people's cars, but the police call it stealing."

"Oh, gosh!" I exclaimed. "And you, Debbie— what did you do wrong?"

"Well, to tell the truth," she confessed, "I suppose I was a bit of a mutt. There was this friend of mine. She worked in a dress factory, machining blouses, skirts, trouser-suits and things like that. You know. Anyway, she got hold of a few extras, as you might say."

"Extras?" I puzzled. "How do you mean?"

"Well, in a big factory, they can't keep check on all the garments that are machined. At least that's what Gloria thought, but it turned out she was wrong. She used to flog them to her pals, see. Fifty pence for a blouse; two pounds for a trouser suit. Well, I ask you? How could I turn down bargains like that?"

"But it's wrong." I looked at Debbie in dismay. "You didn't have anything to do with it, did you?" Then I remembered she had. She'd already passed on some of the stolen property by giving Molly the poncho. *My friend Gloria who works in a dress factory got it for me cheap.*" Those had been her very words.

" 'Course I did," she said now. "It was all too good to miss." She glanced down at her slim-fitting jeans. "Where do you think I got these, and most of my other gear? Oh, I grant you our step-father is a money-bags, but he doesn't hand out unlimited lolly. So I was a bit tight for money to spend on clothes, and I've got to keep my end up with the other girls."

"Oh, Debbie!"

"Well, don't look at me like that," said Debbie. "I didn't do the stealing. All I did was to buy the things from Gloria. I paid her all right, but that didn't satisfy the police. They had me up, in the juvenile court for being in possession of stolen property."

"What happened then?" I asked, loosening my grip on the reins as I leaned over to hear every word.

"As I said, I got probation."

I felt stunned. Debbie was so matter-of-fact about it all, as if she was just discussing a bad school report.

Oh dear! After hearing all this I felt that somehow I didn't like Frankie and Debbie half as much as I had done. Now I could understand John's worry for Molly's sake and his distress that they had come back into her life.

It seemed they were a bad example, after all,

particularly as Debbie seemed to take it all so calmly. I felt rather shattered.

If I hadn't been so upset by Debbie's confessions I might have paid more attention to Freckles and I would have certainly seen the big piece of yellow cardboard in the hedgerow and so Freckles' sudden shy might not have caught me so much unawares.

As it was, her sideways jump threw me on to her shoulder and, before I could regain my seat, she set off down the lane at a frightened gallop.

"Steady, Freckles." I struggled back into the saddle and took a pull on the reins, but the strawberry roan fought the bit. Wildly now, she was careering over the uneven surface of the stony road, fleeing from the yellow cardboard that had scared her so much.

"Hold her, Jackie! Can't you stop her?" Debbie called anxiously as she and Jet cantered after us.

Hearing Jet's hoofbeats behind her seemed to frighten Freckles even more. With a sinking heart, I realised she was bolting, and I was unable to stop her.

All too soon, I knew, the lane would reach its junction with the main road and soon we would be among the stream of tourist traffic winding along to Beddgelert, each car filled with visitors eager to see the site of Gelert's grave—

the memorial to the Llewellyn's faithful hound which Debbie and I had set out to visit.

"Steady, Freckles, you silly pony!"

I tried to keep my voice calm to reassure her and crouched over her neck to lift my weight from her loins so as to ease her progress along the stony road.

"Please stop! There's nothing to be frightened of. No need to run away."

I leaned back and threw my weight down in the saddle. Dropping my hands, I brought the pressure on her reins low on either side of her withers and pulled hard down on her mouth, willing her to halt.

Above her flying hoofbeats I could hear the noise of the traffic on the main road just ahead.

"Stop, Freckles!" I put all my strength into the downward pressure on her mouth. "Do stop!"

Freckles' hooves seemed to slow a fraction as we came to the road junction.

Then from the A.A. box at the corner stepped a patrol man, fastening up his yellow oilskin jacket against the sudden shower that had begun to descend.

"Hold hard, missy!" he called, stepping towards us. "This road surface is very slippery just now. You don't want your pony to have a fall."

The man's yellow jacket glistening in the rain

upset Freckles again. She snorted, slid to a sudden stop, and threw me on to her neck.

The man moved to grasp her bridle. Freckles swerved away and the A.A. man slipped on the wet tarmac and went down in the path of an oncoming car.

"Help! Stop!"

I held up a hand to warn the car and, still gripping my reins with my other hand, threshed back my legs, searching for my lost stirrups in an attempt to regain the saddle.

The car hooted as it swerved to avoid the A.A. man and with a frightened whinny, Freckles bolted afresh. She was beyond all control now.

I must have got back into the saddle somehow because Debbie told me afterwards that I'd managed to pull round Freckles' head and turn her out of the path of the traffic into the stone wall that bordered the road. The wall was low but Freckles' hooves slipped on the greasy take-off surface and she came down with her knees hard on the wall while I flew over her head to land on the stony mountainside, knocking myself out.

The next thing I knew I was lying on the grass verge at the roadside and struggling to sit up while somebody kept easing me down again and a woman tried to cover me up with a car rug.

"Keep still, cariad," she was saying in a kindly

Welsh voice. "The ambulance will soon be here."

"I don't need an ambulance."

My head ached though my senses were clear. My body felt bruised but I felt sure there were no bones broken. I flexed my legs and arms, then tried to stand.

"Take it easy, bach," the Welsh woman was saying. "Best go to the hospital and let them have a look at you, isn't it."

"I'm not hurt," I insisted, struggling to my feet. "Where's Freckles? Where's the pony?"

A mournful whinny made me turn my head. A little way off, the centre of a group of people, poor Freckles made a doleful sight. Debbie was holding her head while Jet stood nearby, one leg through her trailing reins. Blood was seeping from Freckles' knees and while I watched a big, capable-looking man was climbing down from a lorry laden with sugar beet.

"I'm a farmer," he said. "Let me have a look at the pony." His expression was concerned as he examined Freckles' legs. "Is this your pony?" he asked, turning to me gravely.

I nodded miserably. I could see that Freckles' cuts were far from superficial. She'd fallen on the wall with all her weight and with the full impetus of the jump behind her. Like poor Black Beauty in the story, she'd "broken her knees". Not that the phrase really meant any bones were broken, of course, but the injuries would take a long time to heal; there might be permanent stiffness and Freckles would be scarred for life.

"You can't ride this pony home, young lady," the farmer said with kindly concern. "I tell you what. My farm's only a mile away. Let me go back there and fetch the pony trailer. Then I can give you and the pony a lift home. This old sugar beet can wait till the morning."

I nodded, too upset to speak.

This was my fault. John had warned us that Freckles was unreliable to ride—yet, somehow, I'd felt that I'd known best.

John had known better. Perhaps with patience and care, and with his expert pony knowledge and horsemanship he might, in time, have been able to re-school Freckles. He'd wanted to try. He'd intended to give her another chance, even to devote himself to re-educating her in what little free time he'd had left when the activities of the trekking centre were over for the day. Now, however much he might improve her, what would her future be?

Like Black Beauty, a pony bearing the scars of broken knees would be known to have fallen badly on a hard surface. People would realise she'd been involved in an accident and who then would be willing to buy her for a child to ride? By my recklessness I'd probably robbed Freckles of all her chances.

I felt Debbie's hand on my arm.

"Don't take it too badly, Jackie." She tried to comfort me. "You think it was all your fault but I'm to blame too. There I was telling you about my lurid past, not thinking how much it was upsetting you. You were so taken aback with what I was saying that you couldn't keep your mind on your riding."

I barely heard what Debbie was saying. At that moment, all my thoughts were about Freckles.

"Oh, Freckles!" My head throbbed as, sick at heart, I leaned my cheek against her sodden neck and, through my tears, stroked and soothed her. "What's going to become of you?"

CHAPTER SEVEN

A MESSAGE FROM MOLLY

At this very moment Freckles' fate is being decided...

I poured my heart out in a letter to Mummy and Daddy that night, writing by torch-light, sitting up in my bunk in the caravan after Babs had fallen into an uneasy sleep.

The light's still burning in the farmhouse kitchen and I can just imagine what's happening there. Molly will be pleading with John for another chance for Freckles, and Susan, perhaps, will be backing her up. Tessa will be trying not to take sides, but deeply feeling Freckles' plight.

Meanwhile here I am, waiting for Molly to come back. I'll know by her footsteps what the verdict has been. If she comes running down the orchard with happy cries, I'll know everything's all right. But if, as I fear, she comes back with heavy steps, hating to break the bad news to us, how dreadful that will be because Freckles' fate will be all my fault.

And Freckles is one of the sweetest ponies in

the world. All her misdeeds are due to fright, and I know, deep down, that she could have so many happy years ahead of her. She'd give so much pleasure and love to understanding owners who had the time and could be bothered to find out what lay behind her fears and panics and to help her to get over them.

I broke off.

I'll have to stop writing now. The battery of the torch is running out and I can barely see the words . . . I can't bear the suspense any longer. I'll put out the torch. Then I'll count to a hundred and go across to the farmhouse and see if they'll let me in to back Molly up.

"Fifty-seven, fifty-eight, fifty-nine . . ."

I never got to sixty. Shame on me! I drifted into a troubled sleep, and, when I woke with a jerk, the luminous dial of my watch showed that I'd been asleep for nearly two hours. It was now twenty-five past one in the morning.

"Are you there, Molly? What's happened?" I whispered as I felt for the light switch.

Babs and I sat up in our bunks, blinking at each other. Our expressions turned to surprise and alarm as our gazes fell on Molly's empty bunk with its coverlet still undisturbed and her Panda pyjama case still neatly in place.

Molly hadn't come back to the caravan.

I plucked back the curtain. No lights shone in the farmhouse. Outside the night was dark for a moment until the moon rode from behind a cloud to spill silver on the orchard and the drowsing ponies.

"Everyone seems to have gone to bed," I said.

"Then where's Molly?" asked Babs, putting a leg over the side of her bunk. "Why hasn't she come back?"

I pulled on my jeans and sweater over my pyjamas. "I suppose it's just possible that she might be sleeping over at the house," I said doubtfully. "But, oh dear, suppose something's happened to her on the way from the farm to the caravan. She hadn't got a torch and the cobbles would be slippery after the rain."

"Gosh! I can just imagine it." Babs hurriedly dressed. "She might be lying there. We'll have to look. Where's your torch, Jackie?"

"The battery's run out," I said.

We stumbled out of the caravan into the darkness, wishing that the moon would come from behind the clouds again to light our way but the night was deeply dark now and there was no more moonshine.

There was only the glimmer of light from the caravan to guide us as we crossed the orchard and made our way over the cobbles to the kitchen door, softly calling: "Molly, where are you?" and then pausing in case there was an answering cry.

Our voices sounded forlorn in the night. We

didn't dare to call too loudly in case we disturbed everybody else.

"Perhaps Molly's gone in to Freckles," Babs suggested. "That's where she might be."

Feeling our way along the wall, we reached the strawberry roan's loose-box.

"Are you there, Molly?" I called softly.

There was no reply; not even the whicker of a drowsy pony from the darkness within. Quietly we opened the door. Somehow the loose-box felt strangely empty. We clicked on the light. Yes, Freckles had gone and, spiked on the hook from which a wispy hay-net still hung, was a piece of paper bearing a hastily-written message from Molly.

Dear Jackie and Babs,

I was going to put this note through the caravan door, but I thought it might wake you up and then you might have given the alarm before you knew what you were doing.

I'm having to run away with Freckles in order to save her. John won't let us keep her any longer. He says what happened yesterday proves she's too unreliable to be safe and even if his conscience would let him sell her nobody would want to buy her with scarred knees.

I'm sure John's going to have Freckles shot. He says it would be kinder than selling her without a guarantee. So I'm taking her somewhere safe to

72

give me time to work out a plan. I'd have woken you up and asked you to help but I knew that wouldn't be fair to you because John would only send you both home when he found out and then he'd probably ban you from Pinewoods for ever.

Don't give the alarm too soon. Give me a chance to get Freckles away.

Yours, in despair, Molly.

"How dreadful!" I said, shattered. "Poor Molly. What a difficult decision she had to make." I broke off. "I don't see how she can take Freckles far with those bad knees. What shall we do, Babs? Ought we to go after her? She must be having a terrible time, all by herself, leading that pony in the dark."

"Well, perhaps she's not far away." Babs was trying to think clearly through her dismay. "She's probably somewhere in the woods, waiting for daylight. Even then she can't take Freckles far without making her knees worse."

"John's sure to catch them quite quickly after he finds they've gone." I shivered. "I don't like to leave Molly to take all the blame. I wish we were with her wherever she is. If only the torch hadn't gone out we might have tried to follow Freckles' hoof-prints and tracked them down."

I turned to my cousin. "Oh, dear, Babs. What do you think we ought to do?" I broke off in alarm and touched Babs' arm warningly as I heard a window in the farmhouse being pushed open. "Quick! Put out the loose-box light," I whispered. "Somebody's heard us."

"Keep quiet," said Babs, "and they'll think it's just the wind. We'll wait for a while until they've settled down. Then we'll creep back to the caravan. We'll have to pretend we've been asleep all night and haven't missed Molly. We've got to give her and Freckles a chance."

Babs and I didn't sleep much that night and although we did eventually drop off we were awakened at dawn by the crowing of the roosters at the farm lower down in the valley.

Trekking days started early at Pinewoods because any stabled ponies had to be watered, fed and mucked out first thing. Then the ponies in the fields had to be given hay and there were twelve or thirteen human trekkers to feed as well as the family and us. Tessa was sure to need a couple of helping hands.

I was just about to thrust my legs over the side of my bunk when I heard Misty and Patch whickering softly in the orchard outside. They seemed to be welcoming someone they knew.

"Perhaps Molly's come back," said Babs sleepily.

I pulled aside the checked curtain to peer out of the window on my side of the caravan. However, it was not Molly who was coming across the dew-wet grass in the rosy light of early morning.

It was John.

"He's carrying something wrapped up in paper," I reported to Babs. "Odd!"

"Come away from the window," Babs whispered urgently. "It won't do for John to think we're watching him."

We heard Molly's brother's footsteps stop as he reached the caravan, we waited for him to knock or call out. He didn't do either. He seemed to fumble with the doorknob.

What was he doing?

I lifted the corner of the curtain and watched John disappear in the direction of the house. Had he changed his mind about something? Perhaps, still thinking that Molly was safe in the caravan, he'd decided to let her sleep late after her upset of the previous evening.

"If we don't report to the stables soon to help with the pony jobs, he'll get suspicious," I said.

I hurriedly washed and brushed my teeth.

"Come on, Babs."

We dressed quickly and, pulling on our gumboots, went to the caravan door. As we opened it something bounced against the handle.

Babs unlooped a package from the doorknob.

"Goodness!" she exclaimed, reading what John had written on the paper. "Look at this."

"Happy Birthday, Molly," I read, taking the

75

package. "Oh, gosh. It's August the eighth—Molly's birthday, and we'd both forgotten. Yet John remembered, and the others will have remembered, too. I expect most of her presents will be on the breakfast table but John wanted her to have this first thing."

"Yes, to make her feel better," agreed Babs, "because she was so upset over Freckles. He's very fond of Molly. I suppose that's why he's so upset over Frankie and Debbie coming back into her life."

"Poor Molly." I shuddered. "Out all night, on her birthday. Running away and so unhappy about Freckles." I looked at my cousin. "Oh, Babs, what are we going to do? We'll have to tell the others that she's missing. Come on."

We hurried to the farmhouse to give the alarm.

"Molly's run away with Freckles," panted Babs as we burst into the kitchen. "She left a note."

John and Susan broke off in the middle of laying the table and Tessa turned from the stove where she'd been stirring a big saucepan of porridge. A pile of presents waited by Molly's place.

As we broke the news, John's eyes went blank and then he dropped his head in his hands.

"Oh, gosh!" He groaned. "If only she'd waited until this morning. I've been awake half the night wondering what we could organise

77

about Freckles. Now Molly's taken her off into the blue without waiting to hear my decision. Dragging the pony round the mountains with those knees isn't going to help, either. If they don't heal well there'll be nothing anyone can do to save Freckles."

CHAPTER EIGHT

SEARCH FOR A PONY

BABS and I waited while Susan telephoned the White Heather only to learn that neither Molly nor Freckles had been anywhere near the dude ranch. Until it was known where Molly had taken Freckles no one could do anything to help. Even Frankie and Debbie, when questioned, hadn't any idea where their sister had gone. In fact they were indignant and alarmed when they heard she was missing.

"Can you blame Molly for running off?" Debbie rounded on John. "I thought it was shocking how you treated her last night, upsetting her so over Freckles."

"Debbie's right." Frankie moved to his sister's side to face John. "Have you got a blind spot or something, matey? Can't you imagine what it's like to be thirteen years old and to be fond of a pony and have some bossy, unfeeling, so-called brother like you saying that it might be kinder to have a pony put down, just because it's blotted its copy-book?" He followed John who had turned away. "You've got to face up to it, chum.

79

You've driven Molly off, and you can't expect Debbie and me to join you in your rotten search, hunting her down like a blinking fox. What do you say, Deb?"

"Yes, it's you and me she needs not this hard-hearted lot," Debbie agreed. "We're her real brother and sister, her own flesh and blood." She turned to Frankie. "So, what about you and me finding her and Freckles on our own and getting them both away from here, where they'll be properly appreciated?"

"Stop this squabbling," put in Susan. "I won't have it."

John nodded firmly.

"Yes, now we've all let off steam let's get down to a bit of common-sense." He spread out a large-scale map on the breakfast table. "Molly can't have gone far, leading Freckles. She must be somewhere within this area."

He divided the map into sections while Susan and Tessa mustered the trekkers and gave them an emergency breakfast—a bowl of porridge and a buttered roll—eaten standing round the kitchen table, while John outlined his plan for the search.

"You've all been here over a week now," he told the trekking party. "You're quite capable of handling your own ponies and so are able to help in the search." He looked round at them uncomfortably. "We've had a bit of a family argument," he explained "Our young sister, Molly, has run off with one of the ponies, Freckles. So we've got to find them. As you already know, Freckles has been injured and this is a mountainous district with difficult going. Some harm could befall a girl in Molly's state of mind so our quest is urgent."

"O.K., John," Frankie said, now regretting his outburst. "Debbie and I will help."

"Right," said John. "Susan, Babs, Jackie, Frankie, Debbie and I will each form a party along with two of the trekkers. Each group will search one of these sections that I've marked on the map. It's uneven ground with gullies and woods and moorland so every inch of it has got to be covered. Now, don't forget—if you can get to a telephone box, phone back here every two hours or so to report. Tessa will be staying behind at headquarters."

After we'd each studied our territory, John folded the map and put it in his pocket. Then he allocated the trekkers to the various parties and we went to saddle up. I took Misty and Babs rode Patch. Two brothers, called Green, were to go with Babs while Miss Althea Turner—a jolly middle-aged woman with wispy grey hair tucked under a felt hat—and fair-haired Peter Rylands came with me.

"Don't forget to telephone back to headquarters every so often," were John's last words to us all as we set off.

My section lay in the direction of the old lead mines, and as we trotted along the forestry road we were all three watching the ground ahead. Peter noticed hoofprints on a piece of soft ground. They were too big to have been made by Freckles. They were more like the prints of a fifteen hand horse.

We covered the ground slowly, following each side-path, looking along each ravine. As we crossed the moorland, we came in sight of the chimney-stack of the derelict lead mine. Nearby stood an empty cottage and a group of farm-buildings. Could Molly and Freckles be hiding there?

Hopefully we urged our mounts to a trot.

"Molly!" I called. "Are you there, Molly?"

There was no answering shout and no whinny from Freckles.

We dismounted and, while Althea Turner and Peter searched the outbuildings, I hurried to the tumble-down cottage. Someone had been there. The mud outside the doorstep showed footprints and inside, on the stone floor, lay a bundle of straw-filled sacks. In the fireplace were the charred embers of a wood-fire, but the late occupant had not been Molly. Empty beer cans and an old pair of sandals told the story of some roaming hippies.

As I hurried back to Misty, Althea Turner and Peter were coming out of the outbuildings.

"She's not here, dear," Althea Turner sighed, remounting her cob. "What do we do now? Go back, or try to find a telephone to ring headquarters?"

"There won't be a telephone for miles," I pointed out. "I think we ought to go on. There's a climbers' hut up on the mountainside above Cerrig Fawr. It's just possible that Molly might have taken Freckles there."

Apparently Babs, with her search party, had been struck by the same idea because, as we forded the stream below the lake and took the pony track leading along the shore to the mountain we heard a thudding of hooves and saw Babs with the Green boys, astride Firefly and Melody, cantering along the soft pine-needle carpet beneath the trees and emerging on to the grass on the far side of the lake.

"Hey, there," I yelled. "Any luck?"

Babs checked Patch for a moment while she half-turned in the saddle to answer.

"No sign of Molly," she called. "We'll meet you at the end of the lake. Hurry up!"

So, with Peter pushing Darkie, the Exmoor, to the limit of his speed, and Miss Turner's cob lumbering beside Misty, we galloped over the springy turf.

The sun had not yet climbed above the mountain ridge and showers of dew were flung from the grass by our ponies' hooves.

We reached the end of the lake and reined up by the old boat-house just as Babs and the Green brothers came into sight round a clump of larches. They were going slowly now and as we watched, Robert Green brought Melody to a walk. We heard the dragging clop of a loose shoe as they crossed the weed-grown gravel beside the broken-down jetty.

"I don't think I ought to ride Melody any farther," he said, dismounting. "She's got a loose shoe. She could easily get an over-reach."

"And I think we ought to find a telephone," said Althea Turner. "John was most insistent about our keeping in touch with headquarters."

"I suppose there's no need for us all to go on," I said. "But I do think someone should ride up to the climbers' hut to see if Molly's there."

"I'm going back with Robert," said Jeremy Green. "It's no good having a plan of campaign unless we stick to it. Don't forget to telephone back to Pinewoods as soon as you've checked the hut."

"I'll go on with Jackie," volunteered Babs. "Why don't the rest of you ride back? Melody will be out of action unless you can find someone to fix her shoe and Tessa will start worrying if two of the search groups fail to report."

With Robert leading Melody, the others set off in the direction of Pinewoods. Then Babs and I turned Misty and Patch to the mountain.

We tackled the stony track at a brisk trot but soon the path narrowed and curved to follow the contour line—a mere shelf cut out of the mountainside with the ground dropping steeply to the valley. We let Misty and Patch slow their pace to a walk.

Single-file, we followed the old pony-trail that the lead miners had used. Gradually the track began to climb. Higher we went and then, rounding a shoulder of the mountain we came into sight of the climbers' hut, roughly built of stone and nestling into a hollow with a wind-bent mountain ash and a hawthorn bush for shelter. It seemed to blend into the countryside.

We left the track and cantered down the grassy slope towards it.

"Molly!" we shouted. "Mo-o-o-olly!"

The only answer was the echo of our voices, thrown back to us by the steepness of the mountain above.

Babs jumped off Patch and, handing me her reins, ran to try the door of the hut.

"There's nobody here," she reported a moment later. "No sign of either Molly or Freckles."

I looked at the deserted climbing hut and then around at the mountainside with its damp turf and scatter of rounded boulders left by some glacier thousands of years ago.

I gazed from the boulders to the mountain peak above. My eyes followed the line of the skilfully-built dry stone wall that divided the sheep runs. Up there, a few ewes were cropping the short turf, and near the sky-line, I caught sight of a slim figure struggling to help a pony that did not seem able to get to its feet.

Could it be Molly, and had Freckles collapsed unable to go any further?

I was about to shout when I heard a girl's voice calling on the wind.

"Help! Oh, please come and help."

"We're on our way," I answered.

Although the mountain slope was steep, Babs and I urged Misty and Patch to a canter but already we had realised that this was not the end of our quest. We had come on a false trail.

The girl up there on the mountain who was so desperately in need of help with her pony was not Molly.

Who was she?

CHAPTER NINE

A CRY FOR HELP

"Faster, Misty."

"Come on, Patch."

Babs and I urged our ponies up the steep slope as the girl's shouts grew more desperate.

"Hang on." Babs shouted to the girl. "We'll soon be with you."

The mountainside became shaly. Misty and Patch's hooves began to slip so we had to slow them to a walk. Then we dismounted to lead them up the final stretch.

Suddenly we came in sight of a hollow and there, in the dip, a dark-haired, brown-eyed girl, of about fourteen, was struggling to rescue a bay pony whose hind legs seemed to have slipped through some soft earth into a hole in the ground.

"Thank goodness you've come!" The girl looked at us gratefully. "I don't know what I'm going to do. I can't get Wellyn out. The ground seemed somehow to cave in under us and his hindquarters have sunk into this hole. I think it must be one of the air shafts of an old lead mine or something like that. There are a lot of them in these hills."

Babs and I quickly dismounted, ran our stirrup irons up the leathers and knotted our reins so our ponies would not stray.

"Let's see if we can help," I said.

We went nearer to size up the situation. The pony didn't seem to be in any kind of pain and I was fairly certain he wasn't hurt. He looked puzzled as if he were resigned to wait for human beings to get him out of his predicament.

"He struggled at first," said the girl. "Then he seemed to give up, and it's a good thing he did because, if he'd thrashed about too much, he might have hurt himself. As it is I don't think he's injured in any way."

"He certainly doesn't look in pain." Babs gazed at the unfortunate Wellyn. "But we've got to get him out of this fix."

"I wonder how."

I looked at the bay in bewilderment. This was one pony mishap that had never previously come my way.

"I know," said Babs. "If we unbuckle our reins, and make them into traces; then perhaps we can fasten them to Misty's girth and use her to help to pull him free."

I nodded. "Misty's quieter than Patch. So it might work."

While the girl talked reassuringly to her pony, Babs and I got everything ready for the rescue attempt.

My pony Misty flickered her right ear and shifted her feet restlessly as I slipped the reins through her girth, one on either side, and buckled them into place, but she was patient

enough, and even when I backed her towards the unfortunate Wellyn she didn't object. Meanwhile the girl had undone Wellyn's stirrup-leathers and, threading them through his girth in the same way, was able to buckle them to Misty's improvised "traces".

Then she and Babs took up their position one on either side of the pony's head to help to pull him out of the hole and on to his feet. Meanwhile I coaxed Misty forward and the reins took the strain. Would they hold? It was a good thing that I had kept the leather supple, I thought, as they creaked.

"Come on, Wellyn-bach," urged the girl as she and Babs tugged at his head.

"That's it, Misty!" I encouraged. "Another step forward."

The bay's forefeet scrabbled at the ground. We heaved and we tugged, and, at last, he took his weight on his forehand dragging his hind legs unharmed from the hole.

"We shan't come this way again," the girl said ruefully. "I'm going to tell my Dad about this mine shaft, and he'll see that it's fenced off. Dreadfully dangerous, it is."

Babs and I unbuckled our reins from Misty's girth ready to bring them back into their proper use while the girl told us who she was, and how she came to be so far up the mountain with her pony.

"I'm Gwynneth Ellis," she told us. "My Mam and Dad have the farm down there in the valley —Coed Mawr. It means the big wood. This morning Wellyn and I were helping my Dad to look for sheep. We were riding over the mountain. Somehow sheep often seem to get themselves into pickles of one sort or another. Then they're missing and you have to find them. We didn't expect Wellyn to get into trouble this time, or my Dad would never have gone round the far side of the mountain with the dogs, and left me to cover this part on my own."

She looked at Babs and me gratefully.

"Goodness knows what I'd have done if you two hadn't come along. Lucky for me it was; but

whatever were you doing here? Two of the trekkers, aren't you, from Pinewoods or the White
Heather? It would be Pinewoods, I suppose, as
you were calling out for Molly."

"Do you know Molly then?" asked Babs.
"Have you see her this morning?"

The girl shook her head. "I haven't seen her
for more than a fortnight. Very excited she was
then because she'd got two pen-friends coming
to stay. I suppose that would be you two. But upset she was at the same time. She wouldn't say
why but I had an idea she kept falling out with
her brother John."

"Yes, and now she's run off with Freckles," I
said, quickly putting Gwynneth into the picture.
"John said it might be kindest to have Freckles
shot if we couldn't find any other solution. It
was dreadful."

I shuddered as I remembered how Freckles'
fall had come about all because I'd been foolish
enough to think that I knew best and that I could
handle the pony when everybody else but Molly
had failed.

"So Molly's taken her to a place of safety. I
suppose." Gwynneth's brown eyes looked thoughtful. "Now I wonder where that could be. She'd
know she couldn't bring her to our farm because
my Dad would have been sure to have 'phoned
John thinking he'd be worried. Now where in the
world could she have gone?" She broke off and

then her face lit up as a thought struck her. "Animal Valley. She might have taken the pony there."

"Animal Valley," I echoed. "What's that?"

"It's nothing much more than an old cottage with some fields, only a few miles from here. You must have seen it on the telly. A famous book has been written about it called: *Take Not Our Valley.*"

"Yes," nodded Babs. "I remember reading about it and seeing it on the goggle-box when they wanted to flood the valley for a dam for water for Manchester." My cousin turned to me. "You saw it too, Jackie. They took all the animals down to the cottage in the valley. Sheep, dogs, goats, donkeys, calves, cats, hens."

"And so they couldn't flood the valley without drowning all the animals," added Gwynneth, "which would have caused a world-wide outcry."

I nodded as it all came back to me. "It's run by a young couple, isn't it?"

"That's right," said Gwynneth. "Welsh they are; and we're all proud of them."

Babs looked at me excitedly. "Gwynneth could be right, Jackie. Molly could have taken Freckles there."

"Where is Animal Valley?" I asked Gwynneth. "Is it far away?"

"It's only a couple of miles from here," said the Welsh girl. "In fact if you ride down the other side of the mountain," she pointed to the track leading over the ridge, "and follow the path that leads beside the wall, you can't go wrong. It'll bring you down to the old water-mill and there, on the other side of the road, you'll see a gate with a nameboard. *Animal Valley* it says—*no strays turned away*. You can't go wrong, bach. But, just to make sure, I'll come part of the way with you. Wellyn's all right now. There's not a scratch on him. He's only suffering from fright. A bit of a ride will help him to get over his shock."

With high hopes Babs and I mounted Misty and Patch and followed Gwynneth as she led the way down the steep trail to Animal Valley. We leaned forward as our ponies slithered down the shaly places.

As we came to the lower slopes, the path straightened out and Gwynneth said "goodbye" to us and turned Wellyn for home.

CHAPTER TEN

ANIMAL VALLEY

"WE haven't seen any sign of your friend."

Nia Davies looked up at Babs and me as we stood at the door of the cottage in Animal Valley.

"No one's been here all morning. Oh, try to keep still, Marmaduke!" she broke off, gently to push the paw of the black-and-white cat she was holding into the bowl of warm, salty water that stood on the floor beside her. "This cat's got a deep thorn in his pad. I'm trying to get it out for him."

"Perhaps if I held him," Babs volunteered, passing Patch's reins to me.

"No need to," said Nia with a smile, pulling out the thorn. "Here it is. I've got it."

Shaking his wet paw, the black-and-white cat walked a few dignified paces from the bowl before sitting down and began to wash.

"Gwynneth says you're wonderful with all animals," I said, "and I can believe it. If only you could have Freckles."

Between us we told her the sad story of the strawberry roan. While we were talking, Nia's husband, Hugh, joined us. Both listened sympathetically.

Nia's brown eyes looked sympathetic as we talked, and we knew how deeply she must love all animals.

"If only we could have the pony," she said and there was longing as well as sympathy in her voice. "The trouble is, though, we're wondering how much longer we're going to be able to carry on with all the animals we've already got."

"It costs so much to feed them all, you see," explained Hugh, "and people can't afford to help much any more. Money is tight all round these days. So we've had to make a rule—and I've had to be very firm with Nia here about it—we can't accept any more large animals without an endowment, forty pounds for each pony or donkey."

Nia looked up at her husband pleadingly. "I think we could make an exception for Freckles, Hugh."

"No, Nia," Hugh said firmly. "I wouldn't allow it. Where would it all end? Bankrupt we would be if you had your soft-hearted way—and homeless, all the other animals. Tragic it is, but, today, I will have to paint out the sign 'No strays turned away'."

"I'll tell Molly and the others when we get back," I said hopelessly.

"Yes," said Hugh. "Tell them they could pay the money by instalments if that would make it easier. Now, come in, and we will give you some lemonade. You must be thirsty after your long ride."

"May we telephone Pinewoods first?" I asked. "We were meant to phone in every two hours, but just couldn't find a phone box in these hills."

We were soon through to Pinewoods and to our astonishment it was Molly who answered the telephone.

"Goodness!" I gasped. "How long have you been back?"

"About an hour," said Molly. "You see, at daylight I realised Freckles couldn't walk any farther. So I took her straight to the vet and asked him to keep her until her knees were better."

"Running up a fine bill, too," we heard John's voice in the background. He took over the phone from Molly. "Now listen here, you two," he said. "You were given instructions to telephone back hours ago. We were just about to send a search party for you. As if we haven't had enough searching already to last for a long time. Come back to Pinewoods immediately."

Before I could reply, John slammed down the telephone. Babs grinned wryly. "Don't worry, Jackie. Poor John has a lot to put up with at the moment."

"Would you like to look round Animal Valley before you go?" Nia asked us.

"I wish we could," I said, gazing across the farm-yard to the Jersey cow and her calf in the field behind the buildings and the assortment of ponies, donkeys and horses dozing under the chestnut trees, whisking the flies away with their tails as they stood.

"We must go now," said Babs, "but we'd like to come another time."

So we dragged ourselves away, mounted our tired ponies and turned their heads towards Pine-woods.

There, Molly gave us a big welcome and be-latedly we wished her a happy birthday.

"We've forgotten to buy you a present," said Babs. "If you like we'll give you the rest of our pocket money instead. It can go towards the vet's bill for Freckles."

As we watered Misty and Patch, Frankie and Debbie joined us and we told them about our meeting with Gwynneth and our visit to Animal Valley.

"Forty pounds to save Freckles," Frankie exclaimed, putting his arm round Molly. "Chicken feed! If that's all it would cost, Moll, to make you happy again, your troubles are as good as over."

That was before lunch and immediately afterwards, Frankie hurried off without saying a word to anybody or even confiding in Debbie as to where he was going. The last Babs and I saw of him was hitching a lift from a timber lorry as it rattled down the lane.

Tea-time came and still Frankie had not come back; then supper-time. The trekkers had a sing-song in the orchard with Misty and Patch interestedly looking on, but there was no Frankie to accompany them on his guitar.

Twice the telephone rang and Debbie rushed to answer it. Neither of the 'phone calls was from Frankie.

Molly and Babs and I wanted to wait up for him. However Tessa wouldn't let us.

"You three need your sleep," she said firmly. "Off to the caravan with you. Any news from Frankie will keep until tomorrow."

Debbie came across to wake us up next morning.

"Frankie's still not back," she said. "But don't dawdle. The day's work's got to go on, according to John. He wants you to help me to muck out the four ponies from the White Heather. So buck up."

Ten minutes later Babs and I were busy with the shovels and skips, while Molly and Debbie forked the dirty straw on to a wheelbarrow and spread out the clean to the corners of the boxes.

"I wonder where Frankie's got to," mused Babs, stopping for a breather.

"I wonder too," said Debbie. She looked

thoughtful. "I think he'd have made for our step-father, Maxie, for starters; but if Maxie had come across with the money, he'd have been back by now. He must have had to try some other angle."

"Such as what?" asked Babs, helping Molly to pile more dirty straw on the barrow.

Firefly turned her head and whickered, wanting a fuss, so I moved to her side and stroked her neck while we talked.

"I don't really know," said Debbie. "I just hope he hasn't tried anything silly like putting money on a horse or the dogs—or even worse—" She took the wheelbarrow by the handles and pushed it through the loose-box doorway and because, I think, her anxiety was making her exasperated, she added: "Oh, don't keep on, all of you. Can't you see that I don't know whether I'm coming or going? I'm so rattled."

Babs and I looked at each other. We'd never seen Debbie like this before. Usually she was as carefree as her brother Frankie.

Just then Molly who had gone to fetch another bale of straw, ready to start on Jet's box, came running across the cobbles.

"Frankie's back!" she called excitedly. "Look!"

With Debbie in the lead we ran and gazed towards the lane where we could hear the pop-pop of a motor-scooter and see Frankie riding it to-

wards the farmyard. Feet on the ground, he bumped open the gate with its front wheel.

"Frankie!"

Dropping the stable implements, we all ran to meet him and Molly was first to be at his side.

"All your troubles are over, Moll," Frankie said breezily, unbuckling the strap of his orange and black skid-lid and pushing the helmet to the back of his head. "Frankie the Wonder Boy, has fixed it all!"

"Did Maxie cough up then, Frankie?" Debbie asked.

"Well, I tried our big-handed, open-hearted step-father," Frankie said with a chuckle, "but there was nothing doing there. He told me straight that we were already costing him more than he'd reckoned on—and he was thinking about putting us both to work, so I didn't press the matter."

As we watched, Frankie broke off and, with a flourish, pulled a roll of notes from his pocket. "How's this?" He waved the fivers in front of Molly's admiring gaze. "I had a hunch and acted on it and there was enough to buy this scooter as well as pay Freckles' vet's bill and her entrance fee to the home for happy gee-gees!" He handed the money to Molly. "Here, bright-eyes! Here's a belated birthday present from a brother who knows how to treat you right."

"Oh, thanks, Frankie. You're wonderful!"

Molly gave him an excited hug, while over his younger sister's head, Frankie tried not to meet Debbie's accusing gaze.

I could see that Debbie was very unhappy about it all.

"Just exactly what *was* your hunch, Frankie-boy?" she asked. "What've you been up to?"

"Just a business deal," Frankie told her breezily. "What a suspicious mind you've got, Deb! Just because a fellow's been in trouble a couple of times—and for nothing more than a high-spirited lark—you don't have to see Borstal ahead every time he pulls off a deal. Give me credit for being a bit smarter than I used to be."

He wheeled the scooter to the side of the farm-house and propped it against the wall. "Now don't bother any more, any of you. I've been up all night and ridden miles. What I want, now, is a wash, a bite of breakfast, and a good long kip."

We watched Frankie, now looking weary, his shoulders slightly drooping, as he sidled through the kitchen door.

Molly turned to Debbie. "You're worried, Debbie. How do you think he got the money?"

"We'll soon know," Debbie said in a defeated tone. "Events have a habit of quickly catching up with our Frankie."

CHAPTER ELEVEN

SOMETHING DREADFUL

"DON'T make a noise outside Frankie's window,"
I warned Babs as, an hour later, we led Misty and
Patch into the yard. "He'll be asleep by now."

A group of trekkers were waiting for us as we
tied up our ponies. John had given Babs, Debbie,
Molly and me the task of demonstrating to the
beginners how to groom a pony. Meanwhile he
and Susan were taking the more advanced riders
for an elementary jumping lesson in one of the
fields.

"Always be sure that your brush follows the lie
of the hair," Babs told our pupils, going to work
with the dandy brush to get rid of the overnight
mud and loose hair from Patch's coat.

She broke off as John strode back from the
jumping field.

"Stand by," he warned us, looking shaken.
"We're going to have a visit from the police.
Have you seen what's coming up the lane?"

We all turned. Debbie gripped my arm as we
watched a dark blue police car drive up the lane
and turn into the farm-yard.

105

"I half-expected this," Debbie groaned. "I felt Frankie had been up to something dreadful."

We waited while two patrolmen with peaked caps got out of the car and walked across to John.

"Are you Frank Rigby?" asked one, consulting a notebook.

John looked indignant. "Good heavens, no! Frank Rigby's asleep in bed in the farmhouse over there."

"I must ask you to take us to him," said the other patrolman.

"It'd be a pleasure," John said grimly, although I could see that he was shocked and upset. "This way, gentlemen."

Molly caught at John's jacket. "Yes you're pleased, aren't you?" she exclaimed unable to control herself.

"Pleased?" echoed John. "Of course I'm not pleased."

"You said 'it would be a pleasure' to take them to Frankie," Molly's eyes flashed.

"I didn't mean it that way, you chump." John put his hands on Molly's shoulders and gave her a gentle shake. "Pull yourself together. Don't make a scene."

"Scene!" said Molly. "I'll make a scene, all right. It's my brother's future that's at stake. Whatever Frankie did is all your fault, John."

"Oh, is it?" John looked hurt. "How do you make that out?"

"Well, whatever Frankie's done, he did it for my sake to get the money to save Freckles." Molly's tone was bitter. "And all you said was that it might be kinder in the long run to have her shot. I hate you."

"Now, now, miss," the elder of the two policemen broke in. "You're not helping by behaving like this."

Molly broke down then, and Babs and I did our best to comfort her.

Meanwhile John, walking off with the policemen, turned to say over his shoulder: "Try to carry on as usual. Jackie will show you how to clean out the ponies' hooves."

I don't think anyone listened very intently as I explained how necessary it was to take regular care of a pony's feet. I showed the trekkers how to run a hand down the leg to the fetlock before gently lifting the hoof and how to use the hoof pick to clean out the inside each day.

It seemed quite a long time before John came out again. Behind him were the two patrolmen with Frankie, fully-dressed, with tousled hair and looking shattered.

As they crossed the yard, Debbie joined them. "You've done it this time, haven't you?" she said facing Frankie who had now lost his bounce and couldn't even look her in the eyes. "I suppose it was a car you 'borrowed' same as before. But this time you flogged it—that's where you got the money for Molly to save Freckles—and you bought the scooter with what was left over."

"Dry up, Debbie," Frankie pleaded. "I'm in enough trouble with the law as it is. I've already made a statement."

"That'll do, miss."

The policeman hustled Frankie to their car.

As he was about to get in, Molly flung herself past the policeman and touched her brother's arm. "I'll stick by you, Frankie," she told him earnestly. "I'm your sister, too, and I'm not ashamed of you."

John turned to the older of the two policemen.

"What'll happen to him?" he asked. "He's already on probation for joy-riding in cars that don't belong to him."

"Well, the magistrates might take the view that there are some extenuating circumstances in this instance," said the policeman, consideringly. "And he's already made restitution—handing over the money and the motor scooter. All the same he did steal a car and sell it, thereby breaking his probation order. I can't really say for sure, but as like as not it'll be a hefty fine or a short, sharp spell in a detention centre. He'll probably be allowed bail. Meanwhile, we'll have to get in touch with his parents."

"There'll be no difficulty there," said Frankie. "Greenways, Wareham Road, S.E.19. That'll find them."

"It's not as easy as that though," Debbie put in, and I could see Frankie turning to her with panic in his face, and signalling to her.

Obviously he did not want her to say anything more.

"It's no use your looking like that, Frankie," Debbie said definitely. "The police'll have to know. Mum'll tell them even if we don't. We may as well give them the information now, so as not to waste their time."

"That sounds sensible, miss," said the older of the two patrolmen. "What is it, then, that you think we ought to know?"

"Our Mum's married again see," Debbie related while the policeman got out his notebook again and prepared to write down the facts. "It's

Mum and our step-father who live at the address that Frankie's given you. They'll have to be told, of course, but so I suppose will our real Dad—"

"Debbie, you idiot!" Frankie looked alarmed. "Why have you got to bring him into it? I'm in lumber enough as it is."

"Because you and I are going to make a fresh start, Frankie-boy." Debbie faced up to her brother. "We can't go on like this with you stealing and selling cars. I know where it'll all lead to even if you don't—robbery with violence, next ... No, Frankie, we've got to make a clean breast of everything and put the police right into the picture. That way you and I can be helped."

"You've got the right idea, miss," said the patrolman. "Now about your real father? Where can we get in touch with him?"

"I don't really know his whereabouts," said Debbie. "But you'll have him on your records. He's been in and out of prison ever since we were born—and I don't want Frankie, or me, too, for that matter, to follow his footsteps. That's why I'm telling you all this."

"Discharged Prisoners' Aid Society will be able to trace him, I expect, then," said the patrolman, making a note. "Can you give me his full name, and do you know where he was last sentenced?"

"His name's Syd Rigby," Debbie told them while the trekkers listened agog, "and when I last heard of him he'd just come out of Wandsworth, though I don't know what he'd done to be in there or where he'd been sentenced."

"We'll find him, though." The policeman closed his notebook. "You've been helpful, miss. Thank you."

As the police car drove away with Frankie, Peter Rylands surprised us all by calling out:

"Good luck, chum. We'll be seeing you, I expect."

"Business as usual. The show must go on," John was telling the trekkers as Babs and I returned the grooming-kit to the tack-room. "There isn't any more time to spend on the jumping and grooming lessons this morning. Tessa's put up lunch packs for everybody so, if you'll all get your ponies, we'll set off on trek."

A quarter-of-an-hour later the posse of Pine-woods ponies was in the farmyard, shifting hooves, tossing heads, nosing pockets and generally impatient to be off as the trekkers mounted.

John turned to Susan. "You lead this morning. I'll bring up the rear. Come on, Debbie, get moving. Molly, you and Babs and Jackie keep in the middle ready to lend a hand if anyone needs it." He swung himself into the saddle and shortened his reins ready to manoeuvre his horse to close the gate after the cavalcade had clattered through. "Off we go."

"I've been so upset thinking about Frankie," Babs confided when we halted for lunch by the Torrent Falls, "that I've hardly spared a thought for Freckles all morning."

"I've been thinking about them both," I said. "Goodness knows what's going to happen to Freckles now. Shall we go over to see her after tea?"

That evening, after the day's trek and when the ponies were unsaddled and turned loose to graze, Molly and Babs and I caught the bus at the end of the lane and got out by the vet's house in the nearby market town of Llanbedr.

I was wearing my new canary-yellow tank top which Aunt Di had promised me for Easter but being pony-involved like me and so having to cope with a lot of animal problems, she hadn't had chance to finish it until that week. It had come in the post, and the parcel had been waiting for me on the caravan steps when we got back from the trek. I'd tried it on and was so upset thinking about Frankie and Freckles that I hadn't bothered to take it off.

Mr Lloyd-Roberts, the vet, was still out on his rounds when we got to the surgery but his son, Mervyn, took us to see Freckles. There she was in one of the loose-boxes that surrounded the stable-yard behind the vet's house, her intelligent strawberry-roan head over the half-door.

She gave a soft whicker when she heard our voices.

Then, as we came into view her ears went back and she shied across the box, thudding into the wall with a crash.

"Goodness!" exclaimed Babs. "What's wrong with her? Why should she shy away like that? She surely can't be frightened of us."

"I think I can explain," said Mervyn. "I've had a theory about Freckles for some days, and what's just happened seems to confirm it. It seems that she's nervous of yellow—oh, I know some people say horses are colour-blind. Well, they may be, but, like all animals, their eyes react to different tones and shades of light."

"And you think she may be able to distinguish yellow in some way," prompted Babs.

Mervyn nodded. "In certain lights—in strong sunshine, for instance—or in rain when the surface glistens—yellow probably, throws back reflected light very strongly. So, to Freckles, under certain conditions, it probably looks quite different from any other colour."

"Perhaps something unpleasant happened to her which she links, in some way, with that kind of reflected light," I said thoughtfully. "Do you think that could be it?"

"More than likely," said Mervyn. "We did have a similar case with a steeple-chaser of my uncle's. It used to shy at any dark, or dull, red or rusty patch on the ground—a piece of sacking, for instance, or a torn paper-bag that had held cattle-nuts. She associated it with blood, I think. Now, with regard to Freckles, she played up over a yellow plastic bucket when I was feeding her."

"Yes, yellow plastic," put in Babs. "That could reflect a lot of light."

"Just as my jumper did in the sunlight," I said, "and that yellow cardboard in the hedge. That was on a sunny day, too. Then it was raining when she bolted at the sight of the A.A. man's yellow oilskins—those were very shiny and glistening."

"It was a yellow plastic bag that upset her on the day when she ran away with Susan," said Molly. She looked at the youth. "Your theory fits in, Mervyn."

"Well, let's find out for sure." Mervyn took off his windcheater and handed it to me. "Put this on Jackie, cover your jumper and then go up to Freckles again."

Zipping Mervyn's blue windcheater up to my neck I walked to the loose-box and offered Freckles an apple. Calmly she took it from my palm and I rubbed the white star on her forehead while she crunched it.

"Now undo the zip of the windcheater and let her see your jumper," suggested Mervyn. "Stand a little to the left where the sunlight catches it."

114

I pulled down the zip to show the fluffy yellow of my tank top. Yes, Mervyn was right.

Freckles backed away with a snort.

"Come on, Freckles," I soothed. "Don't be silly. It's only me."

Freckles stayed shivering at the back of the loose-box and it was not until I zipped up the windcheater again so that it covered my yellow jumper that she allowed herself to be coaxed forward.

"Oh, Freckles." I put my arm over her neck and whispered into her furry ear. "You poor pony! At some time you must have had a bad fright. Perhaps someone wearing yellow was

115

cruel to you, or you might have had a bump from a yellow car."

"If only we could train her to get used to it," said Molly. "Then she might be a perfectly reliable pony and John might agree to use her for trekking again. After all scarred knees don't matter in a trekking pony as long as the injuries have healed right."

Freckles crunched up the last of her apple and turned her head to nuzzle my shoulder.

"Perhaps there's hope for you yet," I said, and crossed my fingers for luck—both for Freckles and for Frankie.

CHAPTER TWELVE

FAMILY FEELING

"To think of it, Jackie," Babs said, looking scandalised as she broke off from saddle-soaping Patch's bridle to glance at her watch. "It's ten-fifteen. By now Frankie will be in the police court."

I nodded, brushing hard at the lining of my saddle. John was a stickler for clean tack and, that morning, he'd decided to have an inspection before we set out on trek. "I dare say Frankie's and Debbie's mother—Molly's real mother—will be there in court, too, and their step-father, Maxie."

"Yes," said Babs, picking up the polishing cloth, "and I shouldn't be surprised if they all come along here afterwards. It'd be exciting if it wasn't so terrible!"

Babs was proved right sooner than we expected. John had just finished inspecting the tack, and we were all about to saddle up and ride off when a sleek white Mercedes turned into the farmyard.

"They're here!" Molly exclaimed, dumping

her saddle on the fence and turning to the car. "Frankie's with them. So the police haven't locked him up yet. Maxie's driving, and—oh—my mother's there, too."

We watched as first out of the car stepped Maxie Walker—the well-known bookmaker who was also Frankie's, Debbie's, and Molly's step-father. He looked brisk and businesslike in an expensive grey suit with a lavender-coloured shirt and breast-pocket handkerchief to match.

Next alighted Molly's real mother, Ruby. She was slim and auburn-haired with towny make-up, high-heeled shoes and a short fur coat.

Then there was Mrs. Collins, John's and Susan's mother, who was also, of course, Molly's foster-mother. She was trying to put a brave face on everything but her usually cheerful expression was replaced by a strained look.

Last came the cause of the dramatic reunion—Frankie, no longer looking quite so sheepish. In fact he seemed quite perky, I thought, as though he was buoyed up the fact that grown-ups were rallying round.

Molly ran to greet her two mothers—Mrs. Collins and Ruby.

Then Mrs. Collins turned to smile at Babs and me and the rest of the trekkers.

"I'm sorry we couldn't all meet in happier circumstances," she said, looking apologetically around. "It's a pity that our family problems

118

should have cast a shadow over your trekking holiday."

"Yes, it's a downright shame," put in Molly's real mother, Ruby. "And I'm only sorry that it's my son, Frankie, who's been the cause of it all."

"Oh, don't pile it on, Ma." Frankie ran an uneasy hand over his carroty hair. He turned to his step-father.

"Well, give 'em the full strength, Maxie. They're all wanting to know what's going to happen to me."

As Maxie spoke we were all trying not to stare at Frankie, hoping to spare his shame.

Maxie, spoke up so that everyone could hear. "We were all in the court this morning when Frankie was brought before the magistrates, and they decided to remand him on bail for a week while they made further enquiries."

"Looking into my murky past," said Frankie, trying to be jaunty. "All my joy-riding and car-borrowing will be taken into consideration. I s'pose I'll be lucky if I don't get life!"

"Anyway," put in Maxie, "don't let Frankie's misfortunes spoil your day. Mrs. Collins and Ruby and I want to have a talk with John and Susan and Tessa, so I suggest that the rest of you go off for your ride."

"What about me?" Frankie asked. "What am I expected to do while you're discussing me in depth?"

"He's welcome to come along with us," Molly spoke up loyally. "Isn't he, Jackie?"

"Of course," I said, feeling sorry for Frankie and realising that he was not really as perky as he was pretending.

"Thanks, Jackie," acknowledged Frankie. "You're a pal."

A few moments later, we all set off, with Frankie bringing up the rear, as though he wasn't sure whether the other trekkers would want his company. Most of his bounce seemed to have gone and now he just looked lonely and forsaken, so we weren't surprised when Molly dropped behind to ride with him to keep him company. We'd gone only a few yards down the lane when I happened to glance round again. Frankie had dismounted and was tightening Firefly's girth.

Engrossed in this task, he was taken unawares by a surprised shout from Debbie.

Riding at the front with Babs and me she had seen a thin-faced man in a shabby suit coming up the lane towards us.

"Look, Frankie," Debbie gasped, pointing. "Our Dad!"

Babs and I blinked at the man who was approaching us. So this was Frankie's, Debbie's and Molly's real father—Syd Rigby, the man who had spent so many years in prison.

Frankie withdrew his head from the saddle-flap and looked down the road as though he was seeing a ghost.

"Cor!" he gasped. "The old rogue himself, in person, come to pay us a visit."

"And it doesn't seem as if it's a friendly visit," Debbie added cautiously, "judging from the expression on his face."

Babs and I exchanged glances. What was going to happen now?

We looked towards Molly. She seemed bewildered. I tried to put myself in her shoes. What were her feelings? After all, this was a really Big Moment in her life. She was about to come face-to-face with her father whom she had not seen since she was a toddler—a father she never remembered.

I moved to her side. "Shall the rest of us ride on, Molly?" I suggested. "That might make it easier."

"No, don't go," pleaded Molly. "I'm—I'm a bit scared."

"Not half as scared as I am," said Frankie as his father quickened his pace towards us. "The old villain looks as though he's on the warpath."

We watched as Syd Rigby stopped in front of our group. He nodded to Frankie and Debbie, and then seemed to search the faces of the rest of the trekkers. His gaze stopped, in recognition, as he noticed Molly's auburn hair, sunny freckles, and clear blue eyes.

"Hullo, Moll," he said in a hoarse voice. "Don't you know me? I'm your Dad. Come on, lass. Let's be friends. I've come a long way to see you."

"To—to—see—me?" Molly faltered not knowing whether to be glad or sorry. "After all these years?"

"Well, yes, in a way," her father said. He looked sideways. "And to sort out our Frankie here."

He took a step towards Frankie who dodged behind Firefly.

"Steady, Dad," Frankie said, frightened. "Give a fellow a chance."

Syd grabbed Frankie by the front of his shirt.

"So you haven't learned by your father's bad example, eh? You feel you can follow in my crooked footsteps, do you? You with all the chances that I never had."

"Stow it, Dad," Frankie begged.

"So, you don't want me to straighten you out in front of all your mates, eh?" said Syd, shaking him again. "Well, come back to those outhouses then where we can be alone."

Syd gave Frankie a shove and, with a series of prods, jerked him towards the tack-room.

Babs and I looked at each other. What now?

From the tack-room we heard Frankie's ex-gaolbird father's voice raised in anger followed by the slap of leather and a yell from Frankie. I

gasped. Syd was teaching his wayward son a lesson.

"We've got to stop him." Molly turned to Debbie in alarm.

"Oh, Frankie's had it coming for a long time— it's all he understands. If you've got Frankie's real interests at heart, you won't interfere."

But Molly threw off Debbie's grasp. "I'm not believing any of that—Frankie stole the car for a good reason—even if it was wrong—to save Freckles." She ran to the tack-room and flung open the door. Inside, a stirrup-leather in his hand, Syd Rigby was advancing again on Frankie, who was cowering in a corner.

"Stop, you must stop," she cried and before her father could move, she flung herself upon his raised arm, pulling it down. Violently, Syd flung her to the ground, but I saw immediately that he regretted what he had done. He now stood bewildered by Molly's fury, as she glared up at him.

"That's right—always violence," she shouted at her father, eyes blazing. She jumped to her feet and caught Frankie by the arm. Frankie winced but she dragged him towards her astonished father.

"To think that I was so happy when I first realised that my own family were going to come back into my life! I felt it was a dream come true, but now it's more like a nightmare. Look what I've got, a criminal father and a criminal brother at each other's throats."

She broke off to take a deep breath.

"Why don't you both pull yourselves together? It's not too late, You, Dad—"

She rounded on Syd who was now looking shamefaced in front of John and the others who had been attracted by the commotion. "Yes, you, Dad—you must have had enough in prison to make you feel you never want to go back inside."

"Ain't that what I've been saying?" Her father demanded. "Ain't that why I set about Frankie, to make sure he doesn't follow me in my bad ways?"

"Thrashing him like you've done won't cure him." Molly's eyes flashed. "It's more likely to make him feel resentful, so that he turns to crime to prove that he doesn't care. And why? *Because he thinks nobody cares for him.*"

Molly grasped Frankie's hands. "You said you wanted to make it up to me because I hadn't seen you all for so long. Well, if you *really* feel like that, the way you can best make it up is to go straight, and keep out of trouble from now on."

She took her father also by the hand and drew erring Syd and Frankie together.

"What I want is for the two of you to be good friends, and both lead decent lives. That will prove that you really care for me, just as I care for you two, and Debbie, as well." She paused to let her words be clearly understood. "Don't you realise, I *love* you all, just as much as I love John here, and all the Collinses. So let's have some real proof of your affection for me."

Syd hesitated. Then he put an arm impulsively round Molly's shoulders.

"That's my gel!" His voice shook with emotion. Molly had got through to him! "If I do manage to keep on the straight and narrow, it'll be because of you, Moll."

"That goes for me, too," vowed Frankie.

Molly kissed them both, and then, for good measure, flung her arms round John who had

125

been standing there, dumb-struck with new found respect for his adopted sister.

"Thanks, John, for everything," she told him. "You were right ninety-nine per cent of the time." She turned to Syd and Frankie. "Now, for heaven's sake, all shake hands, and go indoors to join the others, and let's start being hopeful and happy for a change."

"Good for Molly!" I heard Babs say. "Who'd have thought she'd sort them out so well and truly. She was terrific!"

Later in the afternoon, when we came back from our ride, we trouped into the farmhouse for tea. All the grown-ups including Syd Rigby were there and with them were Frankie, Debbie, Susan, Tessa and John.

Molly's sincere outburst must have already done good because, as we were helping Tessa to get the meal, she told Babs and me that things were going to be different from now on.

At supper, Maxie announced some of his plans for the Collins and Rigby families, so that they could both pull together in future.

"Well, that about wraps it up," said Maxie. "Frankie and Debbie will work hard here at Pinewoods, with just a bit of pocket money. Frankie knows he's lucky because only the prospect of a hard job will deter the magistrates from sending him to gaol. Syd will be given a job in my organisation, and I'll find him lodgings near my office, so I can keep an eye on him."

This time we did cheer, and as our hurrahs died away, Maxie blew a kiss to Molly. Then he put an arm on his wife's shoulder.

"So, boys and girls, on behalf of Ruby and myself, I'd like to thank you all for what you've tried to do to help."

Then, to my surprise he turned to Babs and me.

"With extra thanks to Jackie and Babs," he said, and then he called across to his step-daughter. "You've got a couple of good friends there, Molly."

Babs and I felt happier than we had done for a long time. Then we came down to earth as we realised we still hadn't heard what Freckles' fate was to be.

"What about Freckles?" called out Babs.

"Yes, what's going to happen to her?" I prompted.

"Ponies!" Maxie turned to John. "That's your department, friend."

"Well, most of Freckles' trouble is that she's upset by yellow objects, and we should be able to 'school' her out of that habit," John told everybody. "Her injured knees are mending well. So tomorrow I'm going to have her home."

"Oh, John, you are a brick!" exclaimed Molly. "That's super."

"Mind you, we'll have to re-educate her to

127

accept the colour yellow," added John. "It'll take a lot of time and patience."

"And if you don't succeed," generously offered Maxie, "she can go into happy retirement at Animal Valley, and I'll foot the bill."

"Wonders never cease," said Babs when we were saying goodnight to Misty and Patch in the orchard that evening. "Who'd have thought that John would have agreed to Frankie and Debbie coming to work at Pinewoods?"

"He knew that Maxie was right and that a spell of hard work was what they both need," I said. "And that goes for Syd, too."

Just then Patch thrust his head against Babs demanding attention while Misty gently nuzzled my hair.

We made a fuss of our ponies as dusk fell. Then, lighthearted now, we knew that there were happy pony-days ahead. We linked arms and made our way through the orchard to the lighted caravan to join our friend Molly who had proved to everybody that—as always—love will find a way, with human beings—just as it does with ponies!